UNDER A STAND STILL MOON

ANN HOWARD CREEL

Brown Barn Books
Weston, Connecticut

Brown Barn Books
A division of Pictures of Record, Inc.
119 Kettle Creek Road, Weston, CT 06883, U.S.A.
www.brownbarnbooks.com

Under a Stand Still Moon
Copyright © 2005, by Ann Howard Creel

Original paperback edition

Library of Congress Cataloging-in-Publication Data

Creel, Ann Howard.
  Under a stand still moon / by Ann Howard Creel.
      p. cm.
    ISBN 0-9746481-8-3 (alk. paper)
1. Indian women—Fiction. 2. Women astronomers—Fiction.
3. Prehistoric peoples—Fiction. 4. Chaco Canyon (N.M.)—
Fiction. 5. Forced marriage—Fiction. 6. Chaco culture—
Fiction. 7. Priests—Fiction. I. Title.

  PS3553.R339U53 2005
  813'.54—dc22

                                            2005011733

Printed in the United States of America

DEDICATION

for Melanie

Also by Ann Howard Creel

The Magic of Ordinary Days

Nowhere, Now Here
A Ceiling of Stars
Water at the Blue Earth

ACKNOWLEDGEMENTS

My thanks go to the people of the Pagosa Springs District of the U.S. Park Service, who introduced me to the wonders of Chimney Rock Archeological Area. Special thanks to Florence Lister, author of *In the Shadow of the Rocks,* who provided historical and cultural assistance as well as encouragement. My gratitude will always go to Nancy Hammerslough at Brown Barn Books for taking the book under her wings.

I also want to thank my circle of friends—Nancy, Lynn, and Kristen—and the writer/friends—Claudia, Susan, and Jessica, who always help me through the highs and lows of the writer's life. Finally, my love and gratitude to my family for putting up with it all.

1

SUMMER GIRL

I cannot remember my birth. I am not lucky in that way, although others are. Some of my People have had dream visions of their entry into this world, but I cannot say that I have, or else I would tell you.

Instead, it is Father who has told me the story of my birth many times over. That I entered this world under a Stand Still Moon, a rare season when the Moon halts its course in the sky and rises nightly between the two rock pinnacles, our Twin War Gods. A time sacred to the People, for only the white-haired elders can remember another time when this event occurred before. And that time, too, was a season of blessings.

A gift, Father said, to be born during such a season.

My first name, Born of the Stand Still Moon, served to remind everyone in our village that much would be expected of me, that much honor would I bring to the Waterfall Clan. But I cannot remember those earliest years, when I was kept on the cradleboard within the pithouse walls in my grandmother's care. I remember little of the days when I was still called by that first name. I remember only that when it finally changed, I was glad to be rid of it.

Instead, my memories begin later, and always, when I recall those days, a warm wind blows through my hair, and the fields are full of new corn, and the leaves of the trees are fully unfurled and green.

Always, it is summer.

I am a small girl, not yet as tall as my grandmother's belt, and the days are long and warm with sunlight. Every day I run and play and sit cross-legged on the ground. I feel the soil with my hands and walk barefoot and feel the Earth between my toes. I run past the fields of high corn. I roam the woodlands to pick berries, and I thank the plants for their gifts.

My memories begin in the open spaces, in the canyons that wind between the mesas, down the ravines that weave like a web among the rocks, over blooming meadows that stretch away until they meet the sky. And in those earliest memories, always I wish that summer would never end.

Father said, "Winter always comes, little one."

My brow lowered upon itself when he said those words. "But the storms of winter keep me inside the pit-house."

Father explained, "The Earth, our Mother, must sometimes rest. During winter, she must sleep under a blanket of snow just as our People sleep at night under our blankets of turkey feathers and robes of buckskin."

I sighed. "There is too much quiet time in the winter."

A smile curled on the sides of Father's mouth. "Without winter, the Earth would be too tired for spring and summer. Just as you would be too tired to run and play if you did not rest."

Mother had been listening without speaking. Finally, she sat down before the fire and clasped her hands before her. "Winter is a good time for Grandmother and me to teach you," she said. "We will show you how to make baskets and sew new robes and blankets."

I tried to bring a smile on my face. In the firelight, Father's eyes twinkled at me from across the room, like two bright stars.

I did not like the winter. The short, cold days kept me within walls doing the work of women. Mother and Grandmother said I should be happy for this quiet time, but I was not. And it was not that I did not like their company—only that my legs longed to unravel and run, that my feet must always move.

In the summer, I often stayed out late. I lingered in the river willows even as the daylight began to fade. The evening air lay cool against me like a deerskin bathed in the waters of the river. While everyone else settled into their pithouses, I sat with my legs tucked under my apron and stared into the night sky until the stars opened their eyes, one by one.

Father was not pleased. "Sometimes, daughter, you stay out late, and your family worries for you."

I said, "I'm sorry, Father," and lowered my eyes. But how could he not understand that in the summer months there was so much to see? How could I stay within the walls of a pithouse when summer bloomed all around me?

Our part of the World, my People's World, is full of places to explore. It lies where one land changes into

another, where the desert climbs to meet the high mountains. There we Sky Watchers live, in the most northern and
eastern of all the cities of the World, in a rich land, a land of
many different lands.

We have the river bottoms in our World, where willows
and reeds grow tall and waterfowl nest in thick grasses. We
have canyons, too, where the bittersweet-smelling sage
covers the silt benches, and higher still, on the sunny mesa
tops, scrub oak, pinyon, and juniper forests make a home
for black bear, deer, and elk. We even have tall pines mixed
with pointed firs that grow on the cooler slopes that face
the north.

In the summer, our land erupts with wild creatures
that I love. Rabbits and marmots crawl out of their holes,
and beavers build dams in high meadows. Spotted fawns
scamper up the slopes, squirrels and chipmunks chatter in
the trees, and birds' nests ring out with new songs.

More than any other creatures, I seek out the birds.
Because of the birds, I received my second name, one that
suited me better than the first. And this story I remember.
I remember because as soon as I learned to climb, I took to
the trees to find those creatures that could soar.

One day, I climbed a tree near our village. Our village
sat beside a ravine on the lowest toe of the mesa overlook-
ing the juncture of the river and the creek, a great place to
climb and peer over everything around me. The two tall
rock pinnacles, our Twin War Gods, stood proudly at my
back, and the river flowed in front of me, below. The birds
liked it here too. I climbed as high as I could until I
reached the smallest branches that would hold me. There
I sang with the tiny black-capped birds and the ones with

bright yellow bellies, and the big black-and-blue jays. My cries were much louder than theirs, bouncing off the canyon walls and echoing all the way back to the center of our village.

"We heard the most unusual sound this morning," Father said that night as we sat around the fire to eat a stew of deer meat and white beans.

"Yes," Mother said. "It was like no other I have heard before."

"We looked outside, to the trees, to see what it was," said Father.

"We thought it might be a new bird," Mother said as she passed me the stew. "But the call of this bird was very different, and the echoes were so rich they roused everyone in the village."

I turned my eyes down, into my bowl.

"Grandmother went outside to see what it was. She said it wasn't a bird at all, but my little daughter," Father said. Then he laughed, a sound like the turkeys talking to one another, and I knew he wasn't angry.

Mother's forehead furrowed as she scolded me. "No, not my daughter making a sound in the trees like a crow!" But I saw the light that brightened her eyes.

From then on, my family starting calling me Echo Song, and then later, only Echo. To my relief, the first name I had been given at birth faded into memory, like dreams never remembered, and Echo remained the name I would carry from that day forward. And my brothers no longer teased me about my singing, for even the old ones said I had a gift. Many times they asked me to sing around the fire in the wintertime. But in the winter, my heart held no songs.

Instead, we passed the cold winter nights listening to the stories of the old ones. And what I am going to say may sound as if I were an ungrateful child. I liked to hear the stories sometimes. But the stories were always about other People and other People's adventures. And after a while, those stories only made me miss the warm weather even more. I listened to the tales of the harvest and the hunt, the ceremonies and dances, but I longed to be outside touching the Earth, making my own stories, finding my own adventures. I longed to be running with my brother, following the course of a stream, or looking for the hidden homes of coyotes.

Mother said I was too busy. She worried about me. "You are like the whirlwinds that blow through the village on hot summer days."

And from Grandmother, "You must learn our ways. You must learn to listen to your own stillness."

But how could I be still when I could walk with the wind across a meadow of waist-high grasses or chase a young buck holding a full set of antlers?

The day soon came when even my Father, who seemed to understand me better than the others, cautioned me about myself. He told me I was different from all the other children born to him, that I could change my mood from happy to angry in the time a spark lights in the fire, and that sometimes he could not understand me. Many times he shook his head slowly from side to side when I did not accept all of his explanations without question. He said I must listen to the lessons of the elders, and that I must learn from others, lest I never become wise.

He said, "You must not question the ways of nature. Railing at the storms, the furious winds, and biting frosts and snows will only make you weak. Bright days and dark days are both a part of our Mother Earth."

But I could not stop myself.

I lingered in every last day of the summer season. When the leaves began to turn gold and orange and red, I pretended not to notice. I knew those colors, even though rich and brilliant, signaled the beginning of fall, and that winter was soon to come. I hoped that if I ignored the autumn changes, they would go away, and the next day the world would be green again.

Of course it did not work. The messengers of the Gods who dwell in the sky above were much more powerful than the wishes of a small girl.

As each day grew cooler, my smiles rose not so high on my face. I walked with slow steps. As I watched the animals prepare for winter, I hoped that each cold season would be shorter than the one before. And I hoped that in years to come, the Earth would not grow so tired and would no longer need her winter's rest.

2

GREEN CORN TIME

Of all summer's gifts, I remember best the green corn time.

Late in the summer, the days grew long, and the Sun hung hot and fiery in the northern sky. Even the highest mountain meadows had lost their snow, and the passes were open and filled with lush grasses and tiny flowers—this is the time I remember best.

In the fields, our crops grew tall and fat, fed by summer rains. In the seven villages, spread along the gentler slopes and rare flat, open plateaus to the south and west of the rock towers, the men had time for gambling games and for trading in the courtyards. They traded turkey feather blankets and cotton blankets, tanned buckskin, sandals, and leggings for clothing, bows and arrows for hunting, tools, and even jewelry.

But that idle time ended when, in our fields, the first ears of corn were ready for harvest. The kernels of corn were white and tender and moist in the husk, and the corn stalks stood tall and proud in our fields.

It was green corn time.

Early in the morning just after sunrise, the men began to harvest the fields. They sent the corn, piled high in baskets, up the steep trails to the village courtyards. Because there was much to carry and our fields were far from the villages, children, even the youngest, were allowed to help the men in the fields. I remember well the first time that my brother, Jumping Fish, and I were allowed to join the men. Father gave us a large basket of corn to carry between us up the long trail toward our village. Proudly we struggled along, but the basket soon grew too heavy for us, and we paused to rest.

Our friend, Falcon, came to help us. "I will take your place," Falcon said as he grasped my side of the basket. "for I am stronger than you."

Falcon annoyed me, but I was tired. So I shrugged and let him take my share of the load.

Falcon was best friend to Jumping Fish, and in my mind, a bit too boastful for a boy only a bit older than I was. But rarely did I scold him, because I felt sorry for him. Falcon had no brothers or sisters of his own, and the other children of his clan, the Blue Stone Clan, were much older than we were; they were at the age when they had begun to think of marriage and children on the cradleboard. Falcon spent most of his days playing outside, close to Jumping Fish. But my brother was my best friend, too, and often I did not want to share him.

I skipped ahead of Falcon and Jumping Fish, up the well-worn trail that led from the valley fields to the villages on the higher plateaus. "You may carry the basket," I called over my shoulder. "But I will reach the village before you. I will toss the first ear of corn into the roasting pit."

But as I reached our village, the village by the ravine that sat below the high triangular top of the mesa and the tall rock pinnacles that were our Twin War Gods, I could already hear my mother calling me away from my play. "Echo! Echo!" her voice carried on the still air.

"Yes, Mother," I said as I emerged from the trail into the open courtyard.

Mother and the other women were scraping out the ashes from the firepits that had burned all night until they had become hot. Mother said, "You must learn how to prepare the pits for corn roasting."

I did not want to learn, but Mother took me aside anyway. She showed me how to line the hot pits with green corn stalks and leaves. Soon the men climbed up the paths from the fields, and all the People of the village by the ravine gathered around the fire pit. We took armloads of the unshucked corn that had been gathered and tossed the ears into the huge roasting pit in the ground. Then we covered the full pit with more corn stalks, and then finally, with dirt.

Our Village Priest, who prayed over and lived in the ravine village, began to dance and chant the Going Home prayers. To the spirit of the Eagle, the spirit of the morning star, the spirit of the ancients, the ants and all the animals, he gave thanks for the early, sweet corn and for the life the Gods in this, the Fourth World, had given us. He sang the song that we must always keep inside of ourselves, lest we lose our way—the Song of Creation. Soon we all joined him as he twirled and danced around in a circle, singing the Corn Dance Song.

> *Who, ah, know ye who—*
> *Who, ah, know ye who—*
> *Who was it made it first?*
> *It was the bright rainbow youth,*
>   *Rainbow Youth—*
> *Ay, behold, it was even thus—*
>   *Clouds came,*
>   *And rain came,*
>   *Close following—*
> *Rainbow then colored all!*

I gave thanks with all the others, but already, my mouth had begun to water as I noticed the steam curling up from the ground over the roasting pits. But I would have to wait until sunset, when the corn was fully roasted and the celebration began. Until then, we could only dream of the feast to come—those steaming hot, tender ears passed around for all to share and eat as much they wanted.

My brother, too, was eager for the corn. "We will have no beans today," Jumping Fish said happily from over my shoulder. For all of the recent spring months, we had eaten dried meat, beans, and corn mush. And even into the summer, before this first harvest, our meals had varied little. Perhaps some fresh meat, steamed greens, or other wild-stuffs found in the forest had been added, but nothing to rival the taste of this hot, sweet corn to come.

"I will eat more ears of corn than there are stars in the sky," Falcon bragged.

As usual, Falcon was trying to impress me. "You are too proud, Falcon," I said to him.

Soon I had had my fill of standing about, waiting for the corn to cook. "Surely we cannot waste a day waiting here in the village," I said.

"Yesterday, we found a new canyon to explore, north of here. It leads to another mesa top, one we haven't explored yet," Jumping Fish told me. "Yesterday we found it, while you were helping our Mother with Summer Wind."

Summer Wind. At mention of her name, my face fell. Our infant sister, Summer Wind, was still on the cradle-board, and in my opinion, too much trouble. She had grown fat and wiggly over the long winter months and would soon learn to walk, but Mother had decided to keep her on the cradleboard as is our custom for one more sea-son. Already, the back of her head had changed its shape. It had flattened from many months on the cradleboard. Now she was growing and demanding too much of our atten-tion. She could eat cornmeal mush from a bowl with her fingers, and she seemed to be hungry at all times. She squealed whenever she did not have our full attention.

I had three brothers to help my father in the fields, but no other sisters to help with the women's chores. Therefore I was often summoned to help my mother with Summer Wind or with any other chores my mother or grandmother decided upon.

Waiting for the corn to be ready, Falcon stood at my brother's side, his face bright with the memories of a day they had spent outside in the sunshine. "In the canyon, we followed a porcupine up a steep grade, and when he tried to shove his tail into our faces and stick us with his quills, we jumped away and avoided him." He stood tall. "We were too fast for him."

I lowered my voice so Mother could not hear. "Will you take me there? Take me today?"

Falcon and Jumping Fish glanced at each other. Finally Jumping Fish said, "It is a steep canyon. It might be too rough for you, Echo."

Too rough for me? I put a hand on one hip. "It will not be too rough. Take me there now, and I will prove it to you. I can keep up with the two of you."

But as we started climbing up the canyon wall, I could see the truth in my brother's words. The only pathway at the mouth of the canyon required an upward climb on a bank of crumbling sandstone with only some sharp and ragged rocks to use as footholds. I struggled along behind my brother, while Falcon climbed behind me.

As I climbed upward, my palms and the backs of my fingers stung, and I knew that I had scraped my skin raw on the rocks. I pulled on plants that grew out of cracks in the rocks and dug my fingernails into tiny patches of dirt that clung there. Slowly I made my way upward, and when we reached the top of the mesa, I brushed the sand from my hands and ignored the scratches that marked my skin.

On the top of the mesa, the air was warmed by unbroken sunlight. We immediately fell down on a mat of thick grass and caught our breath. From our vantage point, we could see all the way across the canyon between the new mesa and ours. We could see our sacred mesa with the Great House standing just below the Twin War Gods. Even from such a long distance away, the Great House looked enormous. Its ground level alone held thirty-five rooms, or so those who had helped in its construction had told us.

"What do you think of the inside of those walls?" Jumping Fish asked and nodded in the direction of the Great House.

"Very fine, I am sure," Falcon said. He stretched out and leaned back on his elbows. "Someday I will see."

I snorted. "I don't care to see."

Both my brother and Falcon turned to stare at me as if they didn't believe me.

"I don't," I insisted.

"But the masonry is so fine, the walls so strong and thick. I hear the interior walls are plastered and painted as fine as the best pottery," Jumping Fish said.

Falcon said, "The floors of the rooms are made with mud and deer's blood. They are slick as river rock and dark red in color."

I shrugged. My companions were behaving like fools. "I do not care to think about a place that has no business with me." Jumping Fish and Falcon had no business with the Great House either. They would never go there. A Guard House prevented commoners such as we were from even visiting the place.

"Tell me something," I said. "Promise to tell the truth?"

My brother and Falcon looked at each other. Then Falcon said, "We promise."

I lowered my voice even though no other person was near to hear me. "What do you think of the High Priests that live in that place?"

Jumping Fish and Falcon again looked at each other,

first with apprehension, but then slowly, they began to smile.

Finally Jumping Fish put his nose into the air and held his face as still as stone. "They are very serious, aren't they?"

Falcon joined in. He stiffened his back. "Their thoughts must be of the gravest importance."

I laughed, for I also thought the High Priests too lofty. But then I puzzled, "If we feel this way, then others must feel the same way too. Why does no one speak of it?"

Falcon and Jumping Fish did not answer. They looked around as though someone might be lurking behind a rock, listening to our words. Suddenly, they acted as if they were afraid to say more.

It confused me. Falcon and Jumping Fish and the rest of my People, all of them, welcomed the High Priests and yet, they seemed frightened of them at the same time. Whenever one of the High Priests strode through our humble village by the ravine, the women stopped smiling and laughing and telling their stories. The men turned their backs and quickly returned to their chores. The children stopped running about and stood still, watching them pass.

I did not like this. I wished the High Priests would go back, would return to the Center of the World.

Falcon picked at his sandals. He looked up at the sky and checked for evil Cloud People. "Do you think they can hear us?" he whispered.

I looked to the sky, but I did not see any large clouds where the deceased lived. I saw only a few thin, wispy clouds. "Those are not Cloud People." I lifted my chin.

"Besides, I am not afraid of the Cloud People. Not all of the Cloud People are evil. My Grandfather has passed into their world, and he is one of them."

Jumping Fish nodded and seemed to relax, but he made no more jokes about the High Priests.

I frowned at my brother. "I am also not frightened of the High Priests." I sprang to my feet. My brother and Falcon followed quickly behind me, fast on my heels.

We spent the rest of the afternoon high on the mesa, chirping with marmots and calling out to birds in the tops of the tallest pines. When the time came to return to the village, we descended the same canyon we had earlier come up. But I found going down even more difficult than coming up had been. It was so steep I had to press my chest into the cliff and hold tightly against it, like the plants that grow flat against rocks.

Jumping Fish and Falcon both descended quickly and went ahead. Slowly, one step at a time, I came down. All would be well, as long as I was careful.

Then, as I lowered myself near the end of the steep section, almost to the place where the ground leveled out, I slipped on a crumbling piece of sandstone. I slid the rest of the way down until my feet thumped on level ground. I had landed awkwardly, tilted over to one side, and into a thorny bush. Several thorns pierced my leg and punctured holes deep into my skin. The wounds immediately began to bleed.

Still, I did not cry out. I brushed away the blood and ran to catch up to Jumping Fish and Falcon without mentioning what had happened. Not until we had left the mouth of the narrow canyon, as we broke away and began crossing an open meadow on the way back to our mesa, did Falcon see the cuts on my legs.

"You are injured," he said. He took my arm and led me to a small ravine where he urged me to sit down on a rock at the side of the trickling water. There, at the water's edge, Falcon softened leaves in the stream and he placed the wet leaves on my torn skin.

I looked up at my brother. I tried not to see the worry he held in his eyes, but I could see it there, even if I longed not to. We could not hide this injury that our mother and father were sure to notice. But when we returned to the village, I hid the cuts from my mother's eyes. She was so occupied with the cooking of the corn and with talking and laughing with the other women in the courtyard that she did not notice.

Jumping Fish could not hide his relief. "Come, let's go down to the river," he said with a gleam in his eye.

But I heard my mother call me again just as I began to run away. "Echo," she said. "You must watch the turkeys while I attend to your sister."

My shoulders fell.

Jumping Fish shrugged his shoulders. "Come, Echo," he said. "We will take the turkeys with us."

"Yes." Falcon grinned. "We can run them all the way to the river."

I grabbed my stick, and with my friends to help, we quickly gathered the turkeys that had spread themselves around the courtyards and pithouses and storage rooms during the cooking of the corn. We gathered them together in one noisy, chattering bunch and headed them in the direction of the river. When we reached the water, the turkeys began poking their heads and looking for worms and insects to eat among the thick blades of grass. Falcon and Jumping Fish decided that we should each gather sticks to tie together and make our own rafts to float down the river.

Falcon completed his first. "I will send my raft down the river before yours," he said.

I was busy tying my sticks together, but for a moment I looked up.

When Falcon stepped out into the shallows to release his toy raft, he sank up to one knee in mud he didn't expect. He tried to pull his foot out of the sticky muck, but he lost his balance and stepped forward with his other leg. It, too, sank deep into the mud.

I laughed out loud and pointed. "Your mother will be angry. Your sandals will be ruined."

Falcon shook a finger in my direction. "You are not kind, Echo," he said, and then he pointed upward at the round white clouds that now had come to float in the sky. "And the Cloud People are watching you."

"You do not scare me, Falcon."

I felt something hard land on my arm. I looked down and saw a large clod of mud sticking there. It began to slowly slide down the long line of my arm.

It was my brother, my brother Jumping Fish, who had done the deed. I glared at him through my meanest eyes. I reached into the mud at the river's edge and grabbed a handful of the mud, but I decided to land the first blow on

Falcon, for he had started the fight with his words. The mud clod landed on the front of his loincloth, and Jumping Fish and I laughed even louder.

Falcon threw more mud at me in return, and before long, we had launched into a full battle. We ran about covered with wet, orange-brown mud all the way from our caked hair to the dripping soles of our yucca sandals.

"Echo!" Grandmother's voice rang out.

I turned, still laughing. I saw her standing at the place where the trail emerged above the river, a water jar balanced atop her head. She called out, "What are you doing? Where are the turkeys?"

In our fun, I had forgotten about the turkeys. Quickly, Falcon and Jumping Fish helped me to round them up, but although we looked for a long time, although we searched through all the willows and reeds along the banks of the river, two of the fattest male turkeys we never did find.

I stood before Grandmother with mud drying all over my skin. She shook her head. "You have let the coyotes take them," she said, disappointment in her eyes.

So it seemed I did need to worry about the Cloud People that day. They would know that I had not watched the turkeys. They would know that I, again, played too hard and did not act as a good child. Even throughout the wrestling games and races and dances of the green corn festival held later that night, I could not forget what I had done.

I sat at the edge of the crowd in the big plaza, and I could not lift my eyes. The corn did not taste as sweet as it had in prior years.

I felt a tap on my shoulder. Falcon seated himself beside me. "Here, give me your hand," he said. Into my palm, he poured a handful of chokecherries. "I found them growing in a spot of sunlight on the south slope of the mesa."

I looked at those sweet berry treats as they slid into my palm from his, and I smiled. "If you found them, you should keep them for yourself."

"No," Falcon said as he looked closer into my face. "On this day, they belong to you."

"Will you share with me then?" I asked.

As we ate together, I let the chokecherries soften on my tongue before I chewed and swallowed them. After a few moments of silence, Falcon said, "It was my fault that you lost the turkeys. I fell first into the mud."

"No," I said. "It was your fault because you talked of the Cloud People."

Falcon sat up straight. "We will behave next time."

I poked Falcon in his side. "No, we won't. You will cause Jumping Fish and me trouble, and we will cause you trouble. It is our way."

Falcon smiled, for he knew my words were true.

Later that evening, Mother discovered the cuts in my leg. I tried to explain to her that it was my fault, that I had convinced Falcon and Jumping Fish to let me go with them up the canyon.

But my words did not matter. Jumping Fish was blamed. Father was angry enough to deny him his gift, a new bow he had brought back from his most recent trading mission, a full day's journey down the river. All the while my grandmother made a paste with cooked herbs to cover my cuts, Father would not look at Jumping Fish in the eyes.

Instead, Father worried over me. He gave me a necklace of small blue beads, a gift he had acquired on the trading mission. He tied the string that held the beads about my neck as my grandmother worked on mixing the paste.

"It is the finest piece I found in all the other villages," he said. "I saved it to give to you today, to honor the green corn time." I touched the beads that felt cool and smooth upon my skin.

This seemed a good time to ask. "Father, may I go with you on your next trading mission?"

Often Father went away to visit other villages down the river and on the other mesa tops where he traded his bone and stone tools, as making tools was his craft. Already he was teaching my older brothers how to shape bone into needles and awls and scrapers. They watched as he turned plain stone into knives and arrowheads and polished stone blades. He taught them how to make stone axes and hammers and hammer stones.

During that summer, he had begun to take my two eldest brothers, Shooting Star and Mockingbird, with him. My brother Jumping Fish, however, was still too young to learn the business of trading, and because I, too, was young and female, I could not go. While Father and our brothers went away for the day, Jumping Fish and I watched the fields, and then I was required to help Mother.

She and Grandmother had always found a job for me. They would send me to fetch water, to start the pot of beans for supper, to build a fire, to dress Summer Wind. After our cousins came to take over watching the fields, Jumping Fish was free to run about and have fun with Falcon, while I had to stay behind and help in the pithouse.

Thinking of this, I sighed.

"You are needed here," Father said.

My shoulders sagged.

"Do not cry, little one," Father said as Grandmother began to spread the paste over my wounds. But it was not my wounds that had brought the tears to my eyes.

3

THE LONG WINTER

Winter always comes, just as Father said it does.

The winter of my thirteenth year was the longest of all winters. Even the old ones said it was the worst winter of their memories.

I still recall the day the cold wind came. Just minutes before, I had been searching for berries by the banks of a highland creek, the only sound the noisy cackling of two black-and-blue jays that played on a rock by the water's edge.

Then all at once, the wind began to blow. It roared through the trees and pushed cold air straight through the fabric of my apron. I turned to face the wind and stood very still. It was odd, I thought, much too early for such a chill. Gold and orange leaves still shimmered on the branches of the aspen trees, and berries still waited to be found in the forest.

But the wind did not care. It ripped the leaves from the aspen trees and stole them away in gusts and swirls. In only a few minutes, the aspen, which had been as brightly colored as the noonday sun, became pale and bare like old bones.

That day, the dogs howled for no reason, and our Village Priest heard voices. He walked through the courtyard with his prayer stick before him and his brow creased upon itself. He called a special meeting with the High Priests who lived in the Great House and had more power than he had, and afterwards he stayed late into the night in the Great Kiva, a special place where I was not allowed, where women and girls could not go. A kiva, a round dug-out chamber with a flat roof, entered from the roof and used for ceremonies, was a gathering place for our men. And the Great Kiva was the largest of them all. It sat higher on the mesa than our village but below the path to the Great House. There the Village Priests met with our council of village leaders, talking and praying.

They emerged after days of ceremony with an important decision. The council leaders said we must quickly finish our autumn harvest and prepare for a long, hard winter. They said we must store our corn and beans and dried meat for the whole season, because our hunters might be trapped in the villages all winter long by heavy snow. So the men rushed to the fields and harvested as much corn as they could. They worked until well past nightfall. The women gathered firewood and stored food, even though we had never done this so early before.

The medicine power of the ravine Village Priest was great in those days. As soon as Mother and I had gathered all the roots and berries we could find and brought as many bundles of firewood to the village as our arms could carry, the snow began to fall.

At first, it came in big, soft flakes that fell like pieces of white goose down drifting out of the sky. But soon, the snow changed. It grew heavy, and the air became a thick white stew. I could barely see the path ahead as I carried my water jar up the trail from the river.

I helped my mother fill the heavy water jars and push them against the walls of the storage room. We stacked bundles of firewood into the corners. In the main room of our house, we covered the floor with deep, soft layers of corn shucks and tassels. This layer we covered with a second layer of skins and blankets and thick mats woven of reeds, juniper bark, and yucca fibers. Finally, carrying armloads of firewood, we lowered ourselves down the pole ladder into the pithouse and made a stack of logs so that we could keep a fire burning in the center of the room at all times.

It was hard work, especially for only two women, Mother and me. That winter, Grandmother was too old to work so hard, and Summer Wind was now off the cradleboard and walking well in her first pair of yucca sandals, but still too young to work.

As I worked, I wondered about the rows of corn that had not yet been harvested, about the vines lined with fat bean pods that had not yet been pulled from the fields, about the big yellow and green squash that had not yet been carried into the villages. And then, I thought of my friends, the animals that lived all around us, in the mountains to the north, in the desert to the south, and all along the riverbed, which was a source of life-giving water to us all. What had they done to prepare for such an early snow?

As my eyes traveled away from my mother's directions, she said, "Echo." Her mouth formed a straight line, letting me know that she was not pleased. Therefore, I did not let my eyes wander again until the floor was set and a hot fire burned in the firepit.

That night, the winds screamed at us as if they were angry. Hard pieces of icy snow pecked the walls of the pithouse in a steady rhythm like the beating of a drum. It took many bundles of wood to keep the fire hot.

I could not sleep. Summer Wind lay warm against my side, and her shallow breath fell softly on my neck. Still, my mind would not stop moving.

I closed my eyes and tried to think of happy places, like the Center of our World, where the High Priests had once lived before they came to stay with us. On another windy cold night like this one, Father and Mother had told me about that place.

"A warm place, where the winds flow freely and nothing breaks the light of day," Father had said. "The mountains are in the distance, along the far reaches of the land."

"The Sun is warm from the first light to the last," Mother said.

"Why, then?" I asked. "Why did the High Priests come here from that place?"

My mouth curled down just to think of the High Priests. And I wondered what I could not ask. Why were their faces so stiff and their eyes so stony?

Father's voice grew deeper. "They have come here to study the skies, to make a chart of the days and seasons, a calendar so that we may always plant our crops at the proper time."

Father barely whispered his next words, for he was wise and did not want to offend the Gods by speaking too boldly. "And they gather strength daily from living in the Great House, on the highest point of the mesa, in the shadow of the Twin War Gods."

I asked, "But why did our People have to build the Great House? Why did our People have to cut the timber and mix the mortar and carry the heavy rocks and stones? And yet we do not have those strong walls to surround our families."

My parents did not answer me for many long minutes. My father frowned, and finally, Mother said, "The Priests have brought the power of the Center of our World with them." She leaned forward, in my direction. "In the Center of the World, there are houses so large they hold hundreds of families and wide straight roads leading out to all the big cities, in all directions. The Priests have brought to us knowledge of building and of craftsmanship. They bring the best masonry and pottery of our World. And, most important, they know how to read the sky."

But I still could not understand why anyone would leave a warm place and come to live high on a windy mesa top. I could not understand why all of my People accepted the presence of the High Priests, yet our less powerful Village Priests had always led us wisely before they arrived, without their help. And they had always lived with us, not above us in a higher place.

As I listened to the storm that raged outside, I tried to picture the Center of the World. I tried to picture a place with warm houses bigger than the Great House with no trees to block the light of our Father, the Sun. But as I tried to find sleep, I could not see it, even in my dreams.

The wind blew louder. I tucked Summer Wind's blanket of soft rabbit fur tightly under her side and pulled the turkey feather robe up just under our chins. I remembered the day of Summer Wind's naming ceremony, during the summer Moon before the time of the green corn. On that day, a warm wind had blown so softly it felt like fur upon our faces.

My father and brothers were lucky. They did not move within their blankets for all of the night. But my mother, like me, did not sleep. Many times during the night, I saw her shadow high on the pithouse walls and heard sparks popping in the air as she tended the fire.

At last, I shut my eyes tightly against the sound of the wind and wished hard. I wished to sleep like my brothers, to find the place where dreams begin, where it would always be summer.

4

RED ROPE

I dreamed of summer. I dreamed of the days that stretch back as far as I could remember. And I dreamed of Falcon.

In my dream, a warm wind blew across my face as I sunned myself in a field surrounded by woodlands. Nearby, my brother Jumping Fish practiced with his bow and arrows while Falcon spread his arms wide and ran over the fields to gain speed. As Falcon sped away, he jumped high into the air. He ran back and forth across the field, leaping into the air over and over again.

"You will never fly," I said to him as I stretched my legs over a speckled pink and black rock. Falcon was foolish trying to fly as a bird does, but he had been stubborn about this for as long as I could remember. From our earliest days, I could remember him trying to sprout wings and fly, to discover the secrets of the birds.

"Yes, I will fly," he said. "Someday, Echo, you will see."

I snorted, plucked a yellow flower from the ground, and stuck the stem into my hair. "You are a foolish boy, Falcon."

"Someday, Echo," he continued. "I will fly, and then

you will be proud that you once knew me. You will say that you once knew the famous boy who took to the skies with the bravest of birds."

I pretended not to notice him. Instead I looked at the pines that stood across the canyon and studied the way the wind whipped the spiny limbs at the tops.

After he lost his breath, exhausted from so much running, Falcon came to sit beside me. "Don't you wonder how it would feel to fly? Think of it, Echo. To soar above the Earth with nothing between your body and the surface of our World. Wouldn't it be fine?"

"Hm-m-m," I murmured as I closed my eyes. I tried to imagine flying. I tried to picture the ground gliding far below me as my wings caught an uplift of air. I hated to admit it, but Falcon was correct about this thing. Soon I could feel it, and I understood his fascination. "Yes, it would be wonderful to fly," I told him. "I admire the birds, too. Come, I'll show you something."

I led Falcon away from the open field, into the woodland where the branches of many trees provided the perfect nesting spots for birds. Jumping Fish grabbed his walking stick and followed along behind us.

Beneath the prickly arms of the tall pines, I closed my eyes and listened to the sounds of the birds. All summer I had listened to and memorized the sounds and melodies of each variety of bird. I had practiced until I could mimic their songs, and therefore, when one of them called out, I called back in the same way. Falcon and Jumping Fish stood with me, silent, listening.

The sound came back, just like an Echo, just like my name. The bird had answered me. It had called back to me just as I had called to him. We turned to each other and smiled silently behind our hands. I had done it. I had fooled the birds into believing I was one of their kind.

Jumping Fish soon skipped away. But Falcon stayed behind. He watched my brother disappear out into the bright light of the open field, and then he reached for my hand.

I pulled away. "What are you doing?"

Falcon shrugged and turned his eyes away from me. He had never answered, and as I lay there in that quiet morning after the storm, I wondered why I had remembered this day in my dream, why I had dreamed of the touch of Falcon's hand upon mine.

I arose when the dim light of morning crept through the pithouse roofing and climbed up the ladder to the open roof hatch. I brushed away the snow that had drifted down on the top steps of the ladder.

It was odd that my dreaded enemy, the winter, the thing that trapped me and held my spirit captive for many months, was at times so beautiful. That morning was one of those beautiful times.

As I gazed outside the hatch, I saw fields of purest white powder unmarked by tracks of any creature. Millions of sparkling spots, like the tiny shells the traders brought all the way from the sea, dotted the surface of the snow. The round pithouses and storage rooms of our village rose out of the sea of snow like islands in a quiet lake.

And above it all, to the north and east of the villages, rose our Twin War Gods, our protectors and twin brothers, offspring of the Gods. I looked to them, as was our custom each morning. Snow clung to the deep cracks and crooked crevices that ran up and down the towers, but it would soon be blown away by the relentless winds that whipped over our World. Farther away, the high mountains to the north lay blanketed in winter's white robe. We would not see the gray heads of those tall peaks until summer once again came to the land.

I lowered myself back into the warmth of the pithouse and helped Mother rebuild the fire and make corn cakes for our breakfast. Then I donned my buckskin leggings and cotton robe and tied my warmest feather blanket around my waist with a braid cord. I lined my sandals with grass for warmth and pulled them on. Then I climbed out of the pithouse, stepped down into the snow and then sank through the surface.

Taking my water jar, I trudged through the snow down to the ravine, toward the river. Some of the older boys and the men were also milling about and working their way toward the fields that lay on tiers of sloping land above the river.

I stood quietly and watched as my uncles and cousins checked the fields that belonged to my clan, the Waterfall Clan. I watched as they brushed the snow from the ears of corn not yet harvested and inspected them for frost damage.

As I watched, my heart began to ache. I did not understand why my brothers were allowed to care for the fields, and I no longer could. Until my twelfth year, I had been allowed to go with my brothers, to follow the clan leader, to thin out the corn plants, to pull the weeds that would rob our crops of their much needed moisture, to tend the fires and keep watch so that ravens and crows could not intrude.

But as soon as I had reached my twelfth year, I was made to stop. Not only was I not allowed in the fields, I was not allowed to play in the forest or race across a wildflower meadow. It was no longer considered proper for me to fly like the wind as it whistles through passes, to run as freely as a waterfall flows down from the high country.

Why was I required to change?

"You must play with your brothers no longer," Mother had cautioned me.

"Why, Mother? I don't understand."

She looked at me kindly. "It is time you learned the work of women. You must learn the skills of a good wife."

But I had no interest in such things. I did not wish to cook inside a smoke-filled pithouse when I could be outside in the sunshine. I did not want to carry children about on my back when instead I could run freely on my own.

But I could not challenge my mother's wishes, so during my twelfth year, instead of tending the fields with my brothers, I had learned to shuck corn, to braid corn strings, to make pottery and weave baskets. After harvest, I had learned to turn the corn and beans each day so they would dry properly and could be stored away for winter. I had learned to grind corn into meal, to simmer pots of fresh greens, and to sew hides together with a bone awl and thread made of yucca fiber. I had learned how to dry the medicine plants by hanging them, tops down, on the walls of the pithouse.

I turned away from the snow-covered fields and walked on. When I arrived at the banks of the river, I brushed the snow from a smooth gray stone and sat at the water's edge. Bare cottonwoods lined the riverbank, and the tips of tall brown grasses spiked up through the snow. I watched as chunks of snow and ice passed by in the swiftly moving stream. My breathing slowed as I listened to the music of the river.

But soon my friend, Red Rope, and two other girls, Moon Face and Sunbeam, came toward me. Their chatter broke the silence of the morning and drowned out the smooth tones of the river flowing over rocks.

I did not understand most of the other girls. They always needed to talk. I was content to listen to the water, to hear the sounds of birds, and to smell the piney scents of the forest. But I smiled at them, for Red Rope was my friend. She was the only girl who could sit with me without having to hear her own voice. In the summer, she and I could search the woods and know without speaking which way to go to find the best berries and nuts. When Red Rope spoke, I listened.

The other girls set their water jars down in the snow and stood about on one leg and then the other. They seemed to have nothing important to do, as if they had the entire day to waste.

"Have you heard?" asked Moon Face, a plump girl with cheeks that reminded me of the fruit from the prickly pear cactus. She answered her own question. "The Village Priest says the winter will last until six full Moons have passed."

"He hears many cold winds and sees many deep snows," Sunbeam said. "When the grasses should be high, the land will still be frozen."

Red Rope looked at me and said softly. "He could be wrong."

Red Rope was being kind. She knew how I felt about

the winter. But the Village Priest was almost never wrong. However, I wasn't thinking about myself at that moment. I was thinking about the animals in the forest and the birds in the trees. How would they survive if winter lasted for six full Moons?

I stared at the river as it rushed by. I watched chunks of ice bob up and down on the surface of the water and careen about until they splashed into stones.

"The family of Lone Pine has asked about me," Moon Face said with a smile.

Sunbeam raised her hands to her mouth. Even my friend, Red Rope, moved closer to hear her story.

I sighed deeply. In the dormant times of winter, my People spent much of their time in gossip. Therefore, I wasn't surprised that these girls could hold their tongues no longer. I continued to watch the river as they whispered to each other and giggled behind their hands.

But Sunbeam addressed me. "This year, we are finally old enough to be married, to take a husband into our mother's clan." She stepped around to get herself in front of me. "Wouldn't you like to take a husband, Echo?"

I stared at the brightly colored stones under shallow water along the riverbank.

"No," I said.

It was true. I did not want more women's work to do, more chores to keep me inside the village and the pithouse.

"She is still a baby," said Sunbeam, her lips twisting upward.

"She wants to take care of fields and animals and not her own house and children on the cradleboard," Moon Face said.

I watched tiny sparkles of light as they danced on the crests of waves moving downstream. I watched the swift current moving in the center of the river, watched it send big lumps of ice crashing into boulders, making water splash high in the air.

Sunbeam remained standing before me, nearly blocking my view. "But what if the husband is Falcon?" she said, and then she smiled high on one side of her mouth.

A lump formed in my chest. Why did she mention Falcon? I didn't want to marry him or any other boy. I only cared for Falcon because he was my brother's best friend. And I liked his name. Falcon was the best name anybody could have. Falcons were the fastest birds of all I had studied. They could swoop down upon any number of smaller birds and overcome them in minutes. And they nested in the cracks and crevices of the rock pinnacles that were our Twin War Gods, the offspring of the Sun God, born at the time of Creation.

Falcon was a perfect name.

And I liked the way Falcon strode through the cornfields with his back long and straight. And I admired the way his hair shone like a polished stone in the sunlight, and the way it fell long and loose like the soft strings inside the cornhusks.

Moon Face said, "We have seen you look after him when he goes away to hunt with his father."

"Like a wife looks after her husband," Sunbeam said, and she laughed at her own joke. "Haven't you seen her, Red Rope?"

Red Rope stood quietly for a moment, and then she sat down beside me on the gray stone. "No," she answered.

I was grateful for my friend, Red Rope. She didn't laugh at me because I liked to explore the woods and river bottoms with my brothers. She didn't hold envy in her eyes the way the other girls did. She didn't resent me because I looked different.

Before the summer past, I had not known that I looked different. Until the day that I saw myself in the flat water of a still lake, I had always thought that I looked like the others, only taller and thinner. Mother had told me I was built lean, like the antelope, whereas most of our People were built broad, like the mountain rams.

But when I saw my face for the first time, I realized more. I saw that my nose was straight and long instead of broad and short. That my eyes were wide and deep. That my skin was smooth like the slick stones beside a rushing stream.

Mother had not told me this. But the other girls had seen it for a long time.

Red Rope said my appearance caused them to tease me. She said that the other girls were scared, scared that I would get the best husband, scared that I would marry a man who was a great farmer and hunter, and that they would have to settle for one who was only average.

Just then, I saw a break in the stream of ice that sped down the river. I sprung to my feet and stepped onto a boulder that jutted out from the bank. Quickly I dipped my water jar into the cold flowing water and felt the jar fill instantly. I stood up and stepped down from the boulder.

Not one drop of icy water had splashed on my clothing or my feet. I remained warm and dry, but my jar was full. My work almost done, I lifted the water jar and balanced it easily atop my head.

Moon Face and Sunbeam watched me with envy in their eyes. They knew they would not accomplish that task with such skill.

But I should have been more careful. For envy is a thing to be feared, my grandmother had always taught me. Don't brag, she would say. Don't cause others to be jealous of you.

But I took my leave and strode proudly away anyway.

5

THE HUNT

After the first storm passed, a few days of winter beauty followed—days of bright snow, warm sunlight, and windless blue skies.

But those days did not last. Soon, there came upon us a season of severe storms, one following the other. Day after day we stayed inside our pithouses as the winds howled and blew in drifts of deepest snow.

Red Rope came to visit. Before the warm fire, we waited until my grandmother drifted off to sleep, when her white head nodded down on her chest.

Red Rope whispered, "Moon Face has taken a husband into her mother's clan."

It seemed no one could talk of anything else but marriage these days. "So I have heard," I said, and then I placed another log on the fire.

"Echo," she whispered urgently. I looked at her face. "A boy of the Fish Clan named Gray Rabbit, do you know him?"

I tried to picture the boy.

"He is tall and laughs freely, like the wind."

"Yes," I said. "I know him."

"His uncles have been talking to my aunts. Do you think I should take him as husband?" Red Rope's eyes danced in the firelight as she waited for my response.

"He seems fine enough," I said, and then I stoked the fire with a long stick.

Her face fell. "You do not think highly of him?"

"That is not my meaning. It is marriage I do not think highly of."

Red Rope hesitated. "But I want to marry," she said.

Grandmother stirred. We waited until she took a long, deep breath and went back into her dreams.

I put my hand on Red Rope's. "Then I will celebrate your marriage and the birth of your children."

Red Rope smiled. "I think Gray Rabbit is very fine. He can hunt down the tall elk, and the fields of his family are some of our finest."

Together we studied the flames. Soon Red Rope frowned again. "If you do not marry, Echo, then what will you do?"

I shrugged as I stared into the flames. "I want only to welcome each day as the Sun Father brings his light to the sky in the morning. I want only to thank the Gods for their gifts of warm days and green fields and running water."

Red Rope stared at me. "And that is all?"

At that moment, I remembered my dream, and I remembered the soft touch of Falcon's hand upon mine. "That is all," I said.

That night, another storm from the north swept in. Then the skies cleared for only a day or two between the storms, not long enough to thaw the ice and snow that covered the Earth. The snow remained all around our villages, piling layers upon layers.

Soon all of our People had to make snowshoes to move around outside. We trampled down a spider's web of pathways connecting our villages to places higher on the mesa, such as the Great Kiva—a kiva so big that all the men of the area could fit in it. We made paths to the river and other places of importance. Even the surface of the river froze into a solid slab. At the shallow crossings, we could walk all the way to the other bank on the slippery ice. And we had to chop holes in the ice with stones or melt snow in the sun in order to have fresh water for drinking and cooking.

Our firepits were the only warm things left on the Earth. Big fires burned continually in the courtyards so that the women would not have to stay huddled around the firepits inside our houses. At night I dreamed of the soft sound of summer winds brushing over the Earth and the smell of the ground washed by midday rain. I dreamed that the roofs of our pithouses were piled high with the corn harvest, the kernels changing color as they dried in brilliant tints of red, black, blue, yellow, and white.

But often I slept with worry for our People and for the animals.

The men had to travel farther and farther to find firewood. The many years they had taken trees from the land around the villages meant longer trips to find wood. And vast amounts of wood were needed that winter.

The men spent much of their spare time in the Great Kiva. There they passed away the cold, short days shaping arrows and making feather blankets and weaving blankets from cotton they had obtained in trade. Inside the Great

Kiva, they held their secret ceremonies. Soon Father began to take Jumping Fish to the kiva with him in order to learn the ways of his men's society, as he was fast approaching the days of his manhood.

Women and children were rarely allowed in the kiva, and therefore we spent much of our time bundled around the fires in the courtyards, grinding corn, preparing food, watching after children, and working on one of the many steps of making pottery. I grew bored with all of Mother and Grandmother's lessons, but I did not dishonor them by refusing any of the skills they wanted to teach me.

One day Jumping Fish ran up to me. "Echo, Echo," he said as he took hold of my arm. "The Priests have been studying the skies. The Sun has reached the spot in the sky where it can go no further south."

"Go on," I said, waiting for him to explain.

"Each year, the Sun reaches this place," he said as he struggled to catch his breath. "And now, it is time to turn back the Sun."

"The winter is halfway over?" I asked.

As my brother nodded, happiness sang in my heart, for I knew that now the Priests would begin their ceremonies. And if we had pleased the Gods, and if the ceremonies were successful, the Sun would turn back toward the northern skies and would begin to warm the Earth again.

Day after day, the Priests held the ceremonies with much dancing and chanting and prayer. Then the Sun heeded the calls of our People in their prayers and began to turn back. Every year, we could count on the Priests to lead us in this most important of tasks, and their power had never failed us.

After the winter ceremonies, the weather still remained bitterly cold even though the days were gradually lengthening. Our hunters had been waiting for the weather to grow milder, but now they could wait no longer. Because our meat stores were growing low, the elder men gathered to plan a large winter hunt. They stayed in the Great Kiva for many long hours to choose a hunting leader and pray to the Gods.

Father returned from the kiva and joined the rest of my family as we sat about the fire. "The hunting leader has chosen Jumping Fish to go on the hunt," he announced.

My brother bowed his head in gratitude. He was in his fourteenth year and ready to move beyond the small hunts with our father, ready to go on a large, organized hunt. But the hunting leader and the other elders must also deem him ready. He must be considered worthy of such an arduous journey in the depths of winter.

Father turned to my oldest brother, Shooting Star, who was already an experienced hunter. "You will go also, to show the younger ones the ways of the hunter."

I opened my mouth to ask about our friend, to ask about Falcon. But Jumping Fish was faster than I was. "What of Falcon?" he asked Father.

Father said, "He has also been chosen."

I smiled, for I knew this news would please Falcon. Neither my brother nor Falcon had ever been on such a big hunt before, and I felt happiness for them. But as I pictured them away in the deep woods, longing ached within me.

If only I too could go.

At dawn, the members of the hunting party readied themselves to leave our village by the ravine. A soft wind moved the air, and icicles sparkled in the emerging sunlight. I watched as Falcon, his face glowing, prepared his tools for the hunt. I watched him run his hand down the smooth curve of his bow and touch his fingers to the flint tips of his arrowheads, making sure they were sharp for the kill.

I cocked my head to one side and watched him then place a stone image of a mountain lion into a tiny buckskin bag that hung around his neck. He needed this image to bring luck. Each hunter carried such an image of a hunting animal. Without this and the ceremonial preparations, the hunt could not be successful.

Falcon looked up from his work. He looked through the throng of villagers who had gathered to see the hunters off on their journey and found my eyes. It was as though he had felt my gaze upon his skin. I held his eyes for a long moment, and then I felt a smile push my cheeks up close to my eyes. I felt cold air on my teeth.

Then I remembered. Others stood all around me. All of the older men and those who would remain behind with the women, mothers, and children stood around in a circle in the courtyard to see the hunters off on their journey. Quickly I dropped my eyes and looked to the ground. I kicked the snow beneath my feet as red heat rushed into my cheeks. I could feel my mother's stare upon me. I glanced in her direction. Her eyes were stern and alert, hard, like a scraping tool. She had seen me watching Falcon, and perhaps others had seen me, too.

But I would not be shamed. I took a deep breath, lifted my chin, and looked back at the hunters as if nothing had bothered me. This time, I watched my brothers. I watched how they checked their weapons and prepared to depart. And before the hunting party left the courtyard, I allowed myself one more glance at Falcon. And what I saw surprised me. His face had changed. His eyes glistened, and a small smile pulled on his lips. As he left the courtyard to begin his first big hunting trip, he looked back once in my direction and then turned and strode away.

As they departed, those of us left behind began to sing the Women's Hunting Song:

> *See, we are standing waiting.*
> *See, waiting we stand.*
> *Our Father, the Sun,*
> *We wait for you. We wait for your light.*
> *Now come up. Rise over the mountains.*
> *Give us your light.*
> *Bless our hunt with your light.*
> *Our Father, the Sun,*
> *See, we are standing waiting.*
> *See, waiting we stand.*

In those days, the Gods were pleased with us, for the hunt was successful. Our hunters cornered several deer in a steep ravine close to a waterfall, and then they shot them with arrows. They drove several bull elk into deep snow until they floundered, and the hunters were able to move in on their snowshoes to make the kill. In the forests, the hunters also found mountain sheep, muskrats, otters, badgers, and foxes. They packed the small carcasses and pulled the large elk, sheep, and deer carcasses back to the villages on sleds made of the animals' hides.

When the hunters returned, we women began our work. We skinned the animals and cut the meat into long strips. Then we hung the strips of meat inside our houses to preserve it. In order not to offend our Mother, the Earth, for her gifts were great, we used every part of the animal. All of the meat would be eaten, the hides would be tanned for clothing, sinews would be used for bowstrings, and the bones would be made into tools.

That night around the fire, my brothers told the story of the elk chase to the rest of my family. My brother, Shooting Star, had the honor of telling most of the story, because he was the oldest. As he concluded his telling, however, he frowned.

"Many of the deer and elk have gone south. They have left this high country until spring returns. And those that have remained are thinner than usual," he said. Then he loudly slurped hot corn gruel from his bowl.

Jumping Fish spoke then, "Much of the woodland that once surrounded us has been chopped down and used in our houses or sent down the river to other villages. Some of the animals go hungry. On the trails, we saw their frozen carcasses in the snow."

"We were lucky to find the animals that we did," said Shooting Star.

Jumping Fish added, "The snow is deep this year. Even with our snowshoes, we could move only slowly as we tracked the animals."

We pondered this information. Then Jumping Fish sat up straight, and the expression on his face changed. He said straight to my mother, "Falcon made his first kill today. One of the deer was his."

At the mention of Falcon, my heart jumped into my throat.

Mother nodded slowly as she continued to eat the freshly simmered meat from our cooking pot. In silence, she dipped her baked corn into her bowl.

I wanted my mother to say something, to let me know her thoughts and feelings about Falcon. He could already farm fields. Now he could hunt; therefore he was thought to be a grown man. Once he could provide for a family, he could marry a girl of another clan.

But Mother disappointed me. She remained silent.

I swallowed a bite of the fresh meat, but it stuck in the middle of my throat.

I thought about Falcon, about the way his arms rested smoothly under his hide and cotton cloth robes. A strange feeling came to my stomach when I thought about Falcon, something I had never felt before. It was a good feeling, but also a difficult one. It felt somewhat like being very hungry and having no food, but it also felt a little like having a stomach sickness, when food will only make one worse. I swallowed hard many times, but I could not make the strange feeling go away.

I looked into my bowl. Everything around me was changing, changing too fast for my mind to keep up. The girls of my age were talking of husbands, and the boys were going on big hunts to prove their manhood.

Why must everything change? Why did I feel things that I didn't understand? Why had I stood in the center of the village and not known what to do with my eyes? I didn't know why, but I had an odd feeling that my days of singing with birds and chasing squirrels would soon vanish forever.

6

BEGINNINGS

At last spring came to the land. As the days lengthened, the dead brown brush that covered the Earth blew away in strong winds, and tiny green plantlets began to shoot upward from the snow-moistened soil. Chipmunks came out from hibernation, and even the lizards emerged to sun themselves on the rocks.

As the days gradually grew longer and warmer, the People of my village shed their uncomfortable winter clothing and sat out in the courtyards to take in the Sun's warmth. Mother and I removed all the damp and musty blankets, robes, and mats from within our pithouse and took them out into the sunlight to be aired. Then we swept out the main room with a broom made with small bunches of stiff grass.

Spring was the best time of year for making pottery. Grandmother and Mother insisted that it was time for me to learn, so they took me to the side of a hill where we found good gray-blue clay and brought it back to our village by the ravine in a basket.

We made tempering material by grinding broken pottery pieces until it was as fine as sand. Mother watched my progress as I ground the pottery on a smooth grinding stone. "This is the material of most importance," she told me. "It keeps the vessels from shrinking and from cracking as they dry."

It took days to make the pottery.

Throughout those long hours when we mixed the clay and tempering materials together, in my daydreams I painted a picture of the summer to come. I saw green forests and full streams. I saw butterflies light on flowers and heard grasshoppers hum songs in a meadow circled over by eagles and hawks.

Mother showed me how to roll the mixed clay into long thin ropes.

"Echo," Mother said as my eyes drifted away again on that day. "Now we will coil the long pieces upon themselves to make a bowl."

I watched as Mother shaped the bowl, and then rubbed it until the surface was smooth. After it was fully formed, we set it in the sunlight to dry.

I said, "Shall I fetch water?"

Mother pursed her lips together, but her voice was soft. "You may go now."

I grabbed my large water jar and headed down the ravine to the river. I would go all the way to the full part of the river for water, down the long sloped pathway the women tread all year long. But I would not complain. Many women complained that our villages lay too far away from the river, our permanent water source, but I did not care, especially now. Now I could take my time in fetching the water and spend more time away from my mother's watchful eyes.

When I reached the water's edge, I set down my water jar in the green grass by the bank and watched the water slide by. I listened to the wind in the tops of the trees and watched a red-tailed fox slip in between reed poles making his way to the water.

When I could watch no longer, I stood up and searched the area around me.

That day I disobeyed my mother for the first time. I left my jar and sneaked away to the woods where no other's eyes could find me. I found some wild onion and juniper berries to give to my mother to use as flavoring for soup. But then I puzzled, for she must not know where I had found these treats.

I would have to tell a lie.

I stared at the wild onion I held in my hand until I decided what to do. I would simply tell her I found the onion and berries by the river when I went to fill my water jar, and for this, Mother would be pleased. The onion and berries would add good flavor to her next pot of deer meat stew.

But after I placed the onion and berries in my pouch, I looked all about me and felt a lump form in the back of my throat. I loved these open spaces without walls. I needed to come back. But I was acting against my mother's wishes. And I wondered if the Cloud People had seen me.

When I returned, Mother had been busy hanging strips of deer meat inside the pithouse and seemed not to have noticed how long I had been gone. She simply picked up our lesson where we had left it.

Two days later she showed me how to paint the dried

pottery with slip, and then to decorate the pieces with bold, dark designs.

"Now is the best part," she smiled over at me as she painted. "Now we may show off our artistry."

After Mother painted the bowls and mugs and water jars with dark lines and wavy shapes, we fired all the new pottery, and later Mother would select the pieces that turned out best to display outside on the terraces. Throughout my lessons, Mother sang the Song of the Humming Potter and urged me to join in.

I found singing the most enjoyable part.

Every day, I paid attention as best I could to all of my mother's lessons, but in my heart, I was far away. And from that first day, I began to steal away from Mother and Grandmother. My brothers were the only ones who saw me slip away past the fields and into the woods, but they only turned the other way and pretended not to notice.

As soon as I could, I left the village by the ravine every day, slipped past the fields, and crept away to the places that I loved. And I never saw the Cloud People. Throughout all of those days that I was a disobedient girl, they never descended to Earth or appeared to punish me in any way. Although I had heard about the evil Cloud People almost every day of my life, I started to doubt their existence. I had never seen them roast a bad child and eat it for supper. I had never seen them at all.

Many times, Jumping Fish rushed up behind me as I sneaked away. "You are like a snake in the willows," he said from over my shoulder.

I smiled at this great compliment.

"But you will live like a mole in the pithouse if Mother ever finds out."

We ran into Falcon. And just as before, the three of us explored as we had done so often in the summers of our childhood. We found a green creek bed, and there we sat and felt the cool come out of the rocks. We breathed in the sweet air. We climbed a ridge and in the roaring wind on the ridge top, we chased mountain sheep to the highest point on the mesa.

One day in late spring, I found Jumping Fish and Falcon in the river willows, which had become our secret meeting place. The afternoon was sunny, warm, and windless. No Cloud People drifted in the blue sky. We decided to climb high that day, to see if the marmots had yet emerged from their holes. As always, we breathed shallowly and hid in the cover of the willows until it was safe to proceed.

Eagerness sparkled in my brother's eyes. "Do you think they have seen us?" Jumping Fish whispered.

"No," Falcon replied. "All of our mothers are too busy admiring each other's pottery to notice the three of us."

"Yes," Jumping Fish said. "They are jealous of the woman who is the best painter. She has painted all of her pots with tiny triangles and fine, wavy lines."

I said, "Now our mothers can say that she is a terrible cook." We silently laughed together.

Falcon lifted his head out of the willows and looked about like a badger peers from its hole. Then he signaled for us to follow him. We took the river trail upstream for a while, careful not to show ourselves to those who worked on the fields above us.

We turned and followed a smaller stream that emptied itself into the river. Once there, it was safe to stand up and move openly. All around us, tiny green leaves had curled out of their buds, and the first tender shoots of hundreds of different plants had begun to break free of the Earth. A damp, rich smell hung in the canyon, a smell that reminded me of the hollows where bears sleep.

We climbed higher until we reached the top of another mesa that stood tall, west of our villages. And there we sat upon the cool grass and listened to the whisper of the Earth as she spoke to us. For a moment, we enjoyed the silence, and then Jumping Fish asked, "What of your friend, Red Rope?"

I knew exactly what my brother meant, but I did not want to speak of it. Everyone in our village had been whispering the story. The young man who admired Red Rope, the one named Gray Rabbit, had wanted to marry her. But the elders of her clan, the Spruce Clan, did not find him acceptable. Now Red Rope was brokenhearted, but she could not go against the wishes of her family.

"Is she marrying?" Falcon asked.

"No," I said and looked away.

After a few moments of silence, Falcon said quietly, almost in a whisper, "You are a loyal friend."

I turned and saw Falcon gazing at me. I met his eyes, and there I saw an unusual look of tenderness, a look full of some emotion I could not name. I thought at first that perhaps something had wounded him, that something was troubling him. But in the next instant, he cleared his throat, and the look vanished.

As we had found no marmots yet, Falcon suggested that we try to catch squirrels.

We set cord snares for squirrels among several rock outcroppings and chased grouse that preened about their homes in the thickets. Then we went off to explore a narrow canyon that split the southern side of the mesa and followed a small herd of deer making its way down the ravine to water.

"I will be going on a trading journey soon," Falcon announced as we worked our way through the thick underbrush that grew in the narrows of the canyon.

As he continued to speak, he seemed to move slower. "We will bring back salt from the lake that is many long days of travel to the south," he said. He glanced back at me as I followed him over a small jumble of rocks.

He chose his steps carefully. As we moved onward, we began to fall farther and farther behind my brother, who led the way. Falcon continued, "Then we will travel southwest and trade for black stone and the deep blue stones near the river."

I scrambled over a broad boulder and drew very close. "Will you bring back shells?" I asked.

"Ah," Falcon said with a smile. Shells were the most favored trading item among our People. "We hope to find a village that has obtained them from the sea traders. We will save our best tanned buckskin and fur pelts to trade for them."

I remembered the large colorful shell that one of the High Priests wore on a sinew string hanging from his neck. I thought of the unusual shades that it reflected from the sunlight and how the colors changed like the inside of a flower's throat. Sometimes, it appeared pale like the shades of earliest morning, and other times, it appeared dark like the colors of the sunset. But always, it was like no other thing we had ever seen in our land.

Falcon stopped walking and turned around to face me. His movement was so sudden that I almost bumped into his chest.

"I will trade for cotton, too," Falcon said. "For us, so that I can weave our first blanket."

My brother was far ahead of us, and therefore Falcon and I stood for the first time, face-to-face, alone. He had grown taller over the winter, and his shoulders were at the same level as my chin.

I looked up, into Falcon's face. I was so close I could see the deep black circles in the center of his eyes and the tiny beads of perspiration that had formed along the line of his upper lip. I could see his chest rise and fall with each breath. Then I saw the same strange look reappear in his eyes, the same one I had seen earlier on the mesa top. It was a look of happiness, but also of uncertainty.

My mouth went dry on the inside. I looked down to my feet.

"I can farm my own field, and I am a good hunter. When I show your family that I can also weave as fine a blanket as any other man in this village, then I may approach my uncles in the Blue Stone Clan about arranging our marriage."

I managed to look at Falcon's face.

He continued, "But if you do not agree, I will go and never speak of this, ever again."

I had not wanted to marry. I had not wanted to give up my days as a child playing in the wilderness. I had not wanted to spend my life doing the work of women.

But at that moment, my feelings changed. As I looked at Falcon's face and as I saw his kindness and recognized his goodness, and as I remembered the happy memories we had already shared by growing up together, I changed my mind in one instant.

"When will you leave on your trading mission?" I asked.

"Soon," he said, and then he reached for my hand. I stood completely still, not knowing what to do.

He touched my fingers, and the feeling inside me was as soft as the inside of a rabbit's ear. "Do you wish to become my wife? For if you do not, I will not ask again."

"No, no," I said, smiling and curling my hand farther into his. "I mean, yes, yes, I do."

Falcon's face opened into a broad smile as he held my hand. We stood perfectly still in this way until we heard Jumping Fish making his way back toward us.

Falcon dropped my hand.

"What happened?" Jumping Fish asked as he broke free of the reeds and looked worriedly from Falcon to me.

Falcon turned away then, obviously not wanting to let our secret be known. "Nothing," he said. But his happiness spread across his face. "We are simply not as agile as you."

"Yes," I said, laughing. "You are as swift and surefooted as the mountain sheep."

With this great compliment, my brother puffed out his chest and offered to slow his pace as he led us down the canyon. We followed my brother. I walked through the reeds, made my way over rocks, and jumped across streams just as before, but I was no longer the same person.

Of course I would marry Falcon. Of course we would bring children into this World, into my mother's clan. We had been destined for each other from the moments of our births. He, who had no brothers or sisters, would come to live alongside my mother's clan, with our large family. He would become brother to his best friend and husband to the girl who had loved him for long years without even knowing it.

I thought of all the events that would take place over the next months—Falcon's journey, the negotiations between my clan and his clan over the marriage gifts. I would grind corn for four days in front of his mother's house to show that I would be a good wife. He would set up his loom and weave a blanket to show my family that he would be a fine husband. I would sing the Corn Grinding Song as I worked, and Falcon would sing the Song of the Sky Loom as his fingers worked the thread.

The men of my mother's clan would come together and build our house. First they would cut roof poles and gather stones from the canyon and shape them to fit in the walls of the new house next to my mother's. The women would make the mortar to seal the rocks in place. Then when Falcon's weaving was finished and the house was completed and on the day agreed upon, our families would feast and exchange gifts, and afterward Falcon would move his clothing, weapons, and tools into our new house, with me.

Echo, the girl who never wanted to marry, would marry her childhood friend.

Surely the Gods smiled.

7

DESTINY

A few days later, the High Priests announced that the Sun had reached the proper point in the sky for planting. The men readied themselves for this most important task of the year, the seeding of new crops. First came fertility rites to ensure that the seeds would sprout. These rites were performed with endless chanting and offerings of prayer sticks and corn pollen and perfect ears of corn.

After the ceremonies, Father gathered his planting stick, his plumed prayer stick, and a small pouch of sacred corn seeds. Before he left our house, Mother, Grandmother, and I poured water over him to ensure that rain would fall on the crops.

In the center of our field, Father would follow a planting ceremony as old as the Fourth World. First he went to a well-known spot in the center of our fields. With his stick he dug four holes, each almost a foot deep. The first hole was north of the center, the second was to the west, the third was to the south, and the fourth was to the east. He dug two more holes, one to represent the sky regions and one to represent the underworld. In the center, he knelt and painted a cross on the ground with cornmeal, and then he said a prayer and planted the plumed prayer stick in the center of the cross and sprinkled it with more cornmeal.

Next he moved out of the center and, with much chanting, he selected four grains of each color—yellow, blue, red, white, speckled, and black. Then, still chanting, he moved to the different holes and dropped the seeds, one by one, into the proper hole—yellow for the northern hole, blue for the western hole, red for the southern hole, white for the eastern hole. The speckled corn he dropped into the hole representing the sky regions, and the black he dropped into the hole representing the underworld.

As he worked, he sang the Planting Song:

> *See, I am letting the seed fall on the Earth.*
> *See, I am helping the roots grow in the Earth.*
> *By and by the corn will grow tall,*
> *It will make food for all the People,*
> *And we will all sing and dance and be happy.*

After the ceremony, Father filled the holes and planted four long rows of corn, each one beginning at the center and extending to the four directions. For four days after that, no more planting took place. Father and the other men went through many prayer rituals and offerings at shrines and would not eat forbidden foods or gamble.

At the end of four days, the large planting began. Because the remaining planting had to be finished before the rains came, now even the women were needed to help. Mother and I finished planting the corn seeds with our planting sticks in holes dug almost a foot deep. With the corn, we also planted beans and squash in shallower holes.

And then, the Gods blessed us. They sent the soft, warm, spring rains—the woman rains, to water our fields.

As the corn grew, the older boys and unmarried men set up brush shelters on high points so that they could stay down near the fields and take turns watching over them at all times. They looked out for the crows and rabbits and squirrels that would eat our crops if they could. They kept herds of deer, antelope, and elk from trampling the fields. They burned fires, pulled weeds, and tended to every stalk and vine with the kind of attention a mother pays to her newborn.

Before the trading party left to go south, Falcon among them, Jumping Fish and I managed to sneak away from our work to see him only once before he left. We could only bid him a rushed good-bye in the cover of the willows because, on the day of the traders' departure, a noisy gala was held during which all the People of the nearby villages turned out. And during the ceremonies, Falcon and I could only catch each other's eyes and steal a few smiles between us.

All the People came out of their houses and danced and chanted for the safe return of our People. In recent seasons, some of our traders had encountered bands of nomads who sought to make trouble with them. We prayed that the trading party would not come upon any of those wanderers who had no permanent homes and could not understand our ways.

But I did not worry.

Summer had settled itself kindly upon the land. The corn plants reached into the sky, and the wide leaves of squash plants shadowed the Earth. Bean vines grew along the ground like weeds. The streams and rivers ran to the rims of their banks, filled with heavy run-off from the snows of winter. With the crops growing well, the men had time for dozing in the shade, for trading among themselves, and for gambling.

I offered to find nuts and berries for my mother, to find cactus fruits and medicine herbs, and to carry the water from the river. In this way, I could spend my days away from the pithouse. I was able to run freely across cleared meadows and jump over tree stumps. While Falcon was away on his trading journey, Jumping Fish and I climbed to the tops of mesas and carried on our summer adventures without him.

But although I ran and played and worked as before, I was a changed person. In all of my day's events, I found more joy. Even when doing those things that once I dreaded, those womanly chores, I felt joy. I kept my secret plan for marriage to Falcon deep inside me, but still, some could see. Grandmother saw in the way that only the elders can see, and often, she smiled at me and lowered her eyes, showing me that she approved.

I began to wear my hair in the way that is appropriate for young women of marrying age, in squash blossom style. Mother divided my hair into two sections and drew each one to the sides of my face. She looped each long section of hair upon itself and tightened the loops in the center. Then she fastened the loops just beside my ears. As she worked, my mother's hands were gentle, and she hummed a soft song, like the ones new mothers sing to their babies.

Every afternoon after our day's work had been completed, Jumping Fish and I stole away from the village. Often we
talked of Falcon and speculated about what he might bring
home from his trading mission. Although I had not told my
brother of my plans to marry Falcon, he suspected anyway.
I could see a gladness in his eyes, and thoughts sometimes
registered between us in the air, things we knew about but
could not speak. I longed to tell him, to confirm that his
dearest friend would soon be coming to our mother's clan to
live with us. But for once, I would do something in the proper way. I would wait until Falcon returned from his journey,
until his uncles came to speak to my aunts.

But it was on one of those lovely warm days—the kind
with sunshine that soothed the skin, with wind that sang
with the breath of the Gods—it was on one of those perfect
days that everything was to change.

Jumping Fish and I had been busy until late in the day.
He had worked in the fields and I had helped Mother grind
corn, cook the speckled brown beans, and carry water
from the river. When Jumping Fish and I finally slipped
away from the village by the ravine, the Sun was beginning
to touch the ridges on the western horizon, and the light
had changed from bright white to a fiery gold.

The day was slipping away. As we had little time for
adventure, we stayed close to home. We decided to follow
the line of small pine and fir trees growing back along the
base of the high mesa. There, the trees grew up sideways,
right next to the rocky, steep incline of the mesa wall.

"A falcon," Jumping Fish suddenly called. He pointed
to a dark speck in the sky.

I focused my eyes on the speck and recognized it immediately. "It is."

We watched as the falcon dipped and swooped in the air. We saw it track behind a large bird. It was so incredibly fast that it gained on the other bird instantly.

"It is hunting," my brother said.

We held our breath. "Yes," I said in a hush. "It is a male, the smaller and faster of the pair that is nesting on the Twin War Gods. Let's follow." Hurriedly but silently, we scrambled over some rocks and tried to get a closer look. But the falcon disappeared behind the top of the mesa, and we could no longer see him.

I wanted to see more of that falcon, of the one my beloved was named for, and so I pushed onward. I thought what a lucky day it was, what a lucky sign to see a falcon when all of my thoughts were for the one called Falcon.

Jumping Fish and I continued to skirt the base of the mesa until we found a rough trail once used by deer long before the Great House was built. It looked as if it led to the mesa top.

"Stop," Jumping Fish whispered urgently. "We are just below the Great House. The High Priests will not like it that we have come so close."

"We will be as silent as the mountain lion. Come on," I said and motioned for him to follow me.

We started up the slope, grabbing onto branches and limbs to pull ourselves upward on the steep, slippery sandstone. We had to push ourselves hard to move up the incline.

Finally, we pulled up into a small clearing. There we stopped and caught our breath. From that place, the walls of the mesa rose straight up, parallel to the trees, and we could climb no further.

Just then, we saw the falcon. It circled and dipped over our heads as if to say hello. In its talons, the falcon now held the other bird. Proudly he called the high-pitched shrieking cry that only a hunting falcon makes. It pierced the stillness and echoed from the canyon walls.

Jumping Fish and I smiled into the sky. We continued to admire the falcon's flight and remained fixed to that spot as if in a trance. As the falcon soared and floated above, I closed my eyes, just for a second, and let myself imagine what it would be like to fly like the falcon. I remembered when Falcon had tried to fly as a bird, and I let a little laugh escape from my lips as I recalled those carefree days of our childhood.

But just then, another cry rang out into the still air.

And this cry did not come from the falcon. It was a human cry, a terrified human cry. I turned and looked up to the mesa top as I shielded my eyes from the sunlight.

Out of the sky, falling, falling, was a bundle of cloth.

Slowly, as if in a deep dream, I watched the bundle drop. I took one small step forward and reached out with my hands. With a heavy thud, the bundle landed directly into my outstretched arms.

I turned the bundle over. To my disbelief, I saw, amidst the fine cloth of a tightly woven robe, the face of a child. A live, breathing, now crying child stared back at me.

"Echo," was all my brother could say.

As for me, I could say nothing.

As I stood staring into the face of that child, a great commotion ensued above us. People screamed. Some of the men rushed down the causeway while others quickly began to lower themselves down the steep walls of the mesa using ropes.

Jumping Fish shouted to them, over and over, "The child is safe. My sister, my sister, Echo, has caught the child!"

The events that happened next still seem to me as if in a dream. My shock at what had happened made me not able to remember the details well. I do remember loud calls and shouts and villagers rushing about as if in a great hurry. Their faces held the oddest expressions—looks of fear and joy all wrapped up together as one.

I remember walking up the causeway that led to the high mesa with the child in my arms and my brother at my side. I remember being welcomed by the guard at the Guard House and climbing up higher still, until we reached the Great House.

There, all the old Priests, the young Priests, their families, and children stood quietly outside the walls of the Great House to greet me. The mother of the child wept at the sight of her child and kissed my hand as I placed him into her arms.

"Little Moon," she cooed to him as she held him once again.

All the others bowed to me and murmured their appreciation. They seemed to want to talk about what had happened, to reassure themselves that it had indeed happened and that all was well. It seemed that the child, Little Moon, had only recently begun to walk and had slipped away from his mother's watchful eyes. When he toppled over the mesa cliff, they thought surely he would die.

But die he didn't, because of me. I heard my name whispered over and over.

Echo, Echo. Her name is Echo.

Then as I returned to my village by the ravine, clusters of excited children followed behind me, and women and men stood outside their homes and nodded their heads as I walked by. Even the grandfathers stood still as I passed.

I had never been so noticed before. The weight of all those eyes upon me felt heavy on my skin. Nothing was as it had ever been before. And soon, all I longed for was to go back to being the girl who sang with birds and ran in meadows.

But just as the rivers sometimes change their course, so do the pathways of our lives.

In the days that followed, everyone in all the villages chattered and whispered about what had happened and about me. Children followed me when I went to the river for water and offered to carry my water jar. Everyone asked me how I knew that the child would fall, that he would fall from that exact spot where I could catch him.

When I explained that it was only an accident, that I had not had a vision, that I had not known ahead of time that the child would fall, they seemed not to believe me. They asked me what Jumping Fish and I were doing below the mesa, so near to the Great House. They asked me about my dreams and about my visions for the days to come.

I wanted only for the event to be forgotten, to return to the days when I could move about unnoticed, when I could slip away with my brother and no one other than my own mother would care where I went.

Several nights later, my mother gathered her sisters inside our pithouse. We sat before the fire, a dense stillness hanging in the air. But my mother's eyes—I will never forget the pride that glowed in them as she spoke the words. "A great honor has been bestowed upon our clan, upon our family."

Then Grandmother, the leader of the Waterfall Clan, spoke. "You have been asked for," she said, turning her face to me.

I sat up tall on my heels. "Asked for? What do you mean?"

Grandmother continued, "One of the High Priests, the one they call the Sun Watcher, has asked for you in marriage."

As Grandmother's words hit me, my mother moved next to my side. She said, "My daughter, you have brought a great honor to this family and to your clan." Gently, she stroked my hair. "This has never happened to any of our clan before. We will remain commoners, but you will live next to the Twin War Gods. You will live within the warm, safe walls of the Great House. You will never long for anything. You will always have the best harvest from the fields and the finest of pottery and baskets. You will have the rarest jewels our traders bring from all the corners of the land."

I pushed away my blankets and touched my mother's arm. "Mother, I do not wish to go."

Mother's face showed her alarm. She hushed me and looked around her. "Everyone is watching this house. They are waiting to celebrate this great occasion."

I looked to my grandmother, who listened intently to our conversation. I looked to my aunts, whose eyes held the same expectant look as my mother's.

I gulped hard. "Mother, I want to stay here among your clan just as you did when you married. I want to bring a husband to live here, with us, to become one with our family. I do not wish to live in the Great House. I have never dreamed of such a thing."

Mother took my arm. "Yes, I know. This is such good fortune; one would never dare to dream it."

She wasn't listening. "Mother, there is another, another one whom I love."

Mother raised a finger to her lips. "Do not speak of it."

Quickly I turned to my grandmother. "Grandmother, please don't make me go. Please don't send me away."

Slowly Grandmother clasped her hands before her. Her eyes became as small as pinyon nuts, and she spoke in a deep voice so that others, beyond the walls of our pithouse, could not hear. "Listen to me, Echo," she said. "Listen to me as you have never listened before."

I swallowed again and waited for her words.

"All the People think you a person with great powers now. They think the Gods favor you with the gifts of foresight, of premonition."

She leaned forward as she spoke. "Now, they think those powers a good thing because they have brought good results. However," she lowered her voice to a bare whisper. "If you turn down this offer and bring shame to them, then all the People may begin to think you a person with evil powers. They may begin to fear you as a witch."

I sunk into my blankets. Nothing would be worse than to be thought of as a witch. Witches caused disease and death. They caused floods and high winds and could even keep the rain from falling. If the Priests could not cure a witch, then he or she would be shunned by everyone and perhaps be driven away. In some cases, a witch had even been killed.

Slowly I allowed Grandmother's words to sink into my skin. I sat perfectly still for what seemed like an entire night of lonely dreams.

Father had remained silent. He had only listened to this talk without speaking, for the marriage of a clan woman was the work of mothers, grandmothers, and aunts. But I caught his eye as I sat in my spot before the fire, feeling my entire life dreams float away like snow blowing away in a winter wind.

I was not a person with special powers. I was not a witch. I was only a girl who accidentally happened to save the life of high-born child. But despite the aching in my chest, I knew that Grandmother's words were true. My clan would be dishonored if I turned down the proposal. I and all of my family might be blamed as witches for any bad fortune that ensued afterward. And still, I would not have the one I wanted. If I brought shame to our village, which I surely would, Falcon's uncles would never approve of me to be his wife. Because of one accidental event, all had changed.

Father looked at me. In his eyes, I could see the places that hold tears never cried, the pleading there, and knew immediately what I must do.

I would marry the one called the Sun Watcher, a man I had never met before. I would do it for my father.

My aunts informed the Great House of my acceptance, and over the next few days, the High Priest that I was to marry, the one called the Sun Watcher, sent presents to my family. He sent cotton blankets and shell jewelry and rabbit pelts to my father and brothers. To my mother, he sent a rain sash and a plaited bag worked with intricate angular designs. To my grandmother, he sent fine painted pottery.

On our wedding day, he sent a wedding dress made of the palest white buckskin I had ever seen, and new high-topped, moccasin boots. My mother washed my hair and combed it out so that it lay long and smooth and as shiny as black water all about my face. I donned my wedding dress and new boots, and then we gathered up my few belongings—my clothing, a favorite blanket, and the tiny necklace of blue stone beads that Father had given me in a time that suddenly seemed so long ago.

As nightfall came, all of the lowland villagers followed us in a procession as my family led them upward. I walked, feeling all the admiring gazes of the commoners I had known and played beside all of my life, out of the village by the ravine, through the upper villages, and toward the causeway that led to the mesa top and the Guard House.

Leaving the others behind, my family and I were allowed to move past the Guard House, up the rest of the causeway, toward the Great House. As I walked farther onward, I would not look at the faces that stared as I passed. Instead I held my head high and looked straight ahead as a full Moon, huge, mottled and white, rose out of the darkening skies and put everything into stark, clear, silver light. On the narrow causeway that separated the mesa from the villages below, I walked without studying my steps. Even though the bridge of rock narrowed as we climbed higher, and even though steep walls held me on both sides, I would look only ahead, only at the Moon.

I stared into its craters and marks and swaths of palest blue and imagined myself walking not to the triangle of land that topped the mesa, not to the Great House filled with strangers, with High Priests that I had always feared and resented, but straight into the bright, perfect light of moon and stars.

Still my feet carried me onward, and as I walked, my sorrow slowly descended deep into the center of my bones. I buried the old days somewhere silent inside me as I walked forward into a different life. I remembered my days of deceit. I remembered lying. Surely the Gods were punishing me for my rebellious ways, for defying my elders, for railing against the changing seasons. I would never dream of summer again.

8

THE SUN WATCHER

I met my husband outside the walls of the Great House as the Moon rose above us and bathed the air with powdery light. The one they called the Sun Watcher was an old man, older than my father. His black hair was full of coarse gray strands that stuck up around the shape of his head, like the quills on a porcupine's back, and as he smiled at me, I saw that most of his teeth were missing.

After he greeted me, one of the other High Priests joined our hands and prayed for us that we might be given long lives and great happiness. We dipped our fingers in sacred cornmeal, and then my mother and aunts came forward. They fashioned my hair in the way of a married woman—drawn back to the nape of my neck and folded into a bundle. The older women of the Great House brought out the wedding feast of fresh meat, parched corn, wild fruits, sunflower seeds, and dried berries.

After the feast ended, I hugged my little sister Summer Wind tightly to my chest and felt the warmth of her body, the same warmth I had felt beside me every night since her birth, but which I would never sleep with again. When I said good-bye to my brothers, I tasted salt on their cheeks left by their tears.

The Sun Watcher led me to the Great House that would be our home. As I followed behind him, I noticed features of the Great House that I had not noticed on my first trip to this place, features that I had been too stricken to take in. The construction of the walls was very different from the crude cobble, branch, and earth construction of the walls of the pithouses in our villages. Constructed with an outer veneer surface of coursed thick and thin sandstone blocks, it was masonry work of the finest quality, but I did not care.

The Sun Watcher led me up along the top of the wall and down the ladder into the room that would be my home to share with him. Inside our room, the ceilings were high and the walls were made smooth with adobe and painted with bold designs. The floor had been leveled, smoothed with plastered mud, and hardened like bedrock.

I placed my belongings in one corner of the rectangular room and began to tend to the fire, as was a wife's duty. The Sun Watcher sat on an otter fur blanket on the opposite side of the fire pit.

As I fed small logs to the fire, I felt his eyes land heavily upon me.

Finally he spoke. "Do not fear me, young one called Echo."

I leaned close to the ground and blew on the glowing embers beneath the logs. The flames flickered and caught. The light in the room became brighter.

"Look at me," he said.

I looked up, but I had trouble meeting his gaze. Then I saw him turn his face to one side as if to study me with his best eye. The wrinkled skin around his left eye drew up. "You are one with much beauty," he said.

I removed my favorite blanket from my bundle of belongings and spread it before the fire. Then I sat with my legs curled under me.

"Perhaps you would like to know why I asked for you."

I sat still and prepared to listen.

"It is not because of your beauty." A small chuckle came up from deep within his chest. "And not because you saved the child."

This time I looked at him. "Why then?"

He leaned back into his blanket. "Ah, you see it is a problem of the old ones. I am losing my eyesight." He pointed to his right eye. "Already much of the vision is leaving this one, and someday it will leave forever. Lately I fear that the left one is beginning to go bad, too."

I understood. "So you need a wife to take care of you."

He rubbed his chin as he continued to study me with his one good eye. "And you are not pleased about this arrangement. That I can see."

I stared into the flames, for I did not want to lie.

"You see, when your good deed was brought to my attention, I thought I could reward you by giving you a comfortable life."

"I had a comfortable life."

He paused. "You may return if you wish. You are free to leave at any time."

I smiled. "No, it is not possible. This is my clan's wish. I could not refuse them."

He sat for a few more minutes, regarding me. "Then perhaps we can strike an agreement."

At first I would not answer. I did not want to hear his proposal, for there was nothing he could offer me, nothing that could replace what I had already lost forever.

But soon, curiosity crawled on my skin. "What would be the terms of the agreement?"

He clasped his gnarled hands together. "You will help me as my vision fails, and as I grow older, I will give you something in return."

I looked at him through my lashes. "What will you give me?"

He was quick to respond, his gray eyebrows lifting upward. "What do you want? Jewelry? Pottery?"

I looked at my hands. "No, nothing like that."

"What then?" he asked.

I looked at my palms, at the lines that traveled across them. I thought of the freedom that I had lost, the freedom that could never be replaced, and I wondered what could ever compare to that freedom.

I balled my hands into a fist, and then I answered him. My words came from deep within me, from a place I had not known existed. I blurted out the words. "Power. The power of the Priests. That is what I want." I looked up, directly into his eyes. "Share with me your knowledge of the skies."

The Sun Watcher's face grew longer, and his eyes became small dark beads. I had shocked him with my words. The secrets of the skies were the domain only of the High Priests, taught to them by the Gods.

Then his eyes softened as he regarded me more carefully. "So, I see," he said. "It is a bold request, but one that reveals much about your wisdom. You may or may not have a gift of foresight, but certainly you have other gifts." Slowly he brought his blanket high around his shoulders.

Then he addressed me. "You wish to become my student?"

"Yes."

"Very well," he said as he crossed the blanket in front of his chest.

I could not believe his words. Could he possibly be willing to accept my proposal?

"I will teach you the ways of the Sky God. I will teach you how to find the true directions, how to read a calendar on the horizon, how to predict the events that are often foretold in the sky."

At first I could not speak, not even to acknowledge his offer. It would be unheard of for a girl to know such things. It would be unheard of for a Priest to share such knowledge with anyone except other Priests.

"I will show you how to determine the longest day of summer, the shortest day of winter, the time to clear the fields, the time for early corn planting, and the time to plant squash."

He pointed a finger high into the air. "It can all be seen in the sky, my young one, and in return for your care, I will show it to you. I will teach you all that I know."

I did not hesitate. "Yes," I said. "I will treat you with kindness and feed you good meals. I will keep your house warm during the cold winter nights and act as your eyes when your vision has left you."

He smiled.

"I will make you a good wife if you will teach me these things."

He sat back. "As soon as you are ready, we will begin your apprenticeship."

I did not ask to begin immediately. Instead, the next morning, I walked with the Sun Watcher outside in the sunlight. A cloudless sky arced over the Earth and made a perfect blue background for the orange-pink rock towers of the Twin War Gods.

In the bright light of day, I studied the man who was my husband, the High Priest called the Sun Watcher. I could see that his right eye had almost lost its deep brown color, that instead, in the center of the eye lay a pale white orb, like a tiny hummingbird's egg, and I saw that his bones were crippled with the joint disease that affects so many of our elders.

I sat with him on the smooth stone bench built into the wall of the Great House to face the Twin War Gods, placed there to make observation easy. As we sat and warmed ourselves in the Sun, a gray dog trotted up to us. The dog sniffed the Sun Watcher's hand and before long began to lick his fingers.

"There, there," he said as he let the dog taste his skin with its tongue. "Come closer," he said with a smile that crinkled the skin all over his cheeks.

The dog took one step closer, and the Sun Watcher worked his way down the dog's neck and scratched. He dug his fingers into the deep soft fur of the dog's neck and murmured to him in low sweet tones.

"Is the dog yours?" he asked me.

"No," I answered. "I have not seen this one before."

He scratched the dog's neck a few moments longer. "If he is not claimed, perhaps we could keep him as our pet."

I looked into the eyes of the man that I had wanted to hate, the man that was my husband. "I would like that very much," I said.

Over the next days, I settled into the easy routine that would become my new life. I gathered food from the storage rooms filled with the best goods and foodstuffs paid in tribute by my People to the High Priests. I prepared pots of stews and soups with fresh meats and herbs, and made corn gruel into a hot broth for drinking.

I cooked in pots whose interiors were so smooth they did not catch food particles as I stirred. We ate from pottery finer than any I had ever eaten from before. The pottery I'd used before was rather coarse with a few crude black strokes on untreated gray surfaces, but the pottery of the Priests' was similar to that made in the Center of the World, having smooth white backgrounds painted over the entire surface with intricate black designs.

I was allowed to explore every room of the Great House except for the two Great House kivas that were used solely by the Priests. Once a year, one or two of the Priests' wives would be selected to replaster the interior walls of these most sacred kivas, but this was the only entrance allowed to women and was therefore a great honor.

Daily, I left the high mesa and walked down to the river to fetch water, the only time I left the Sun Watcher's side. Although from the Great House, the trip to the river took an even longer time than it had taken from the village by the ravine, it did not bother me. I enjoyed taking long strides down the narrow rock causeway, letting the wind whip my hair loose from its binding as I walked past the man who stood at the Guard House. Many times I lingered in my former village to talk to my mother and to hear the latest news from members of my clan.

I became a friend to Corn Tassel, mother of the baby who had fallen over the cliff wall and wife to the Priest they called the Rain Dancer. Often she let me help tend to the child, Little Moon. He was a boy full of mischief, as had been proven by his mishap, and he required close watching at all times. In return for my help, Corn Tassel gave me a pitcher with a handle, something I had never seen before, and a new large, bladder shaped jar to store water in our room. Soon she began walking with me as we took our lighter water jars down to fetch water from the river.

"Now that the fields are growing tall, soon it will be time to cut timber," she told me.

"And what will the men build?" I asked. It seemed to me that in this place we had all that we needed.

"It isn't to be for us. Timber is badly needed in the Center of the World, where there are no trees. The Priests plan to direct the men to cut the tallest pines in the area. Then they will float them down the river to the City of Two Rivers, where from there, they must be carried overland."

I had heard of such arduous tasks being accomplished before. Much of the wood needed in the Center of the World had been obtained in this way, through the direction of the High Priests and the labors of my People. And yet they asked for still more.

One day, as I passed through the ravine village, I spotted my brother Jumping Fish. For the first time since my marriage, I found him away from his duties in the fields. In his eyes I saw urgency as he motioned for me to come and talk with him.

"Go on without me," I told Corn Tassel. Then I went to my brother's side and set my water jar down upon the ground.

"How are the fields?" I asked him.

"The corn is waist high. The bean pods are bulging like the fat sides of a beaver."

"That is good," I said.

I waited to ask the question, the thing I wanted so desperately to know.

But my brother answered without my asking. He would not meet my eyes, but his voice was low and quiet, like a wind dying. "The trading party has returned."

This was the news I had wanted to hear, to hear about Falcon, but I could not bear to hear all at the same time.

Jumping Fish continued. "All are back safely."

I felt joy in his safe return, but I could not imagine how his joy would vanish when he learned the news. "Does he know?"

"Yes," my brother answered.

And then, before I cried and shamed myself in front of all the People of my village, I picked the water jar up from the ground, placed it upon my head, and walked away.

9

SKY LESSONS

Back inside the Great House, I found the Sun Watcher sitting on his otter fur blanket, attempting to start the fire.

"It is warm today," I said as I took over the duty of setting the logs in place. "One of the warmest days of the year."

"Ah, yes, my young one. It is." He stretched his legs out before him. "But the pain in my knees does not care. And it is lessened by the warmth of the fire."

After I got the fire burning brightly, I sat next to my husband and began to rub his swollen knee joints. "I will ask Grandmother to teach me how to make a salve to rub into your sore limbs."

The Sun Watcher murmured his appreciation.

"Have you heard the tales that the traders bring back?" he asked.

I gulped and momentarily stopped my work. Then I resumed. "No, I have not."

"Well," he said with a smile spreading across his face.

"It seems a woman among the Cliff Dwellers who live in the west has given birth to three infants at once."

I had heard of twins before, but never three born all at once. "How is that possible?" I asked.

"It is a gift from the Gods. Just as those who are born with a sixth toe or finger are blessed, so these three infants will be blessed."

"Are all healthy?"

"Yes, it seems so. They are small, but growing." He laid his head on the blankets and continued to speak. "We also hear that the deer are numerous in the south, near the Center of the World, although there has been a plague of grasshoppers that took many fields."

As he continued to speak, I was reminded of my grandfather's voice, a sound I had almost forgotten.

"In one of the Desert Villages, almost half the children have died from a fever. Our traders avoided that place for fear of witches."

I looked into the fire. "Were any other troubles encountered by the traders?"

He became more and more relaxed. "Only one meeting with a nomadic band that they think might be guilty of raiding some of our villages. But on the day our traders encountered them, the nomads were skinning rabbits and gave them no trouble."

"That is good," I said. I continued to rub his knees and lower legs until I could hear him take the long, deep sighs that come just before sleep.

"Husband?" I whispered. He grunted softly in reply. "The green corn festival is soon to come. It is my favorite event of the year. Do you think we will be able to attend?"

He took another long deep breath, and letting it out, he said. "If I am not able, then you must go without me. You may tell me about it upon your return."

I took the opportunity to ask for even more. "And may I help my family with the harvest?"

"I should think so," he said just before he closed his eyes.

When he fell into a deep sleep, the kind where dreams come from, I covered him, first with a cloth blanket to protect his skin, and then with a turkey feather blanket to retain the warmth I had worked into his limbs. Then I moved away from the fire because, for me, the heat in the room lay heavy on my chest. I leaned my back up against the cool plaster walls and stretched my bare legs out on the hardened floor.

Near me, my husband slept as soundly as a squirrel sleeps curled up in its hole, and for this, I was grateful. In the light of the fire, his face had softened, like the gray-blue clay of the canyon softens in the sunlight, and I could see a slight upturn on the corners of his mouth as he slept, almost as if he were smiling. As I gazed at him longer, I saw the wrinkled skin around his eyes twitch silently as he dreamed.

I could feel no hatred for this man. This man whose soul was kinder than I had dared to dream it would be, who only wanted to be cared for and attended to in his old age, who desired not to deny me my freedom, and who had agreed to teach me his knowledge of the skies, was not my enemy.

I tipped the top of my head into the wall and looked into the ceiling. Through the hatch doorway above, I could see a patch of blue, the beautiful color that painted the Sky World above us, and I knew that I would make my path. In that instant, I knew that I could make the best of the course I had been given by the Gods, that I would care for this gentle old man until his death, and that I would glean from him as much knowledge as I could until that day eventually came.

Two days later, I asked that we begin my first lesson. Green corn time had almost arrived, and the days were long and warm, and the streams were flowing gently with fresh cool waters from the last of the melted snow in the high passes.

I helped my husband out into the sunlight during the warmest hours of the day. We walked slowly down the causeway and beyond the villages east of the mesa to an open area filled with sunshine. And there he gave me my first lesson. He showed me how to find the true directions using a shadow-throwing pole.

First at his direction, I placed the pole, which was the straightest pole I had ever seen, into the ground. I worked carefully, placing rocks around the base, until the shadow-throwing pole stood perfectly straight against the sky.

"Now place a stone at the end point of the shadow made by the pole," the Sun Watcher instructed as he leaned on his walking stick and watched.

Impatient to know more, I said, "I don't understand what I am doing."

He explained, "As the Sun moves overhead, the shadow changes and moves. You will mark the end point of the shadow throughout the rest of the day. And then tomorrow, you will finish the arc by marking the shadows that fall during the morning hours."

"How does this show the true directions?"

He smiled at me. "Patience, my young one. Have patience, and you will see."

I sat back on my heels and waited for the shadow to change its course. I listened as the Sun Watcher told me more. "It is not possible to determine the directions by observing the horizon at sunrise or sunset because the horizon is not perfectly flat. Therefore, in the Center of the World, we devised another method." He rubbed his chin as he watched me. "Have you not wondered how the Priests have been able to align our structures in the proper directions so accurately?"

I shrugged. In many of the cities of our World, the Priests had always organized the buildings and living spaces on a north-south line. "I thought the Gods told you how to do it."

He laughed. "We believe this knowledge comes from the Gods, yes. But there are tricks to be used. We have determined the will of the Gods by obtaining knowledge, by learning skills. These skills are the things I will teach you."

By the end of the afternoon, the stones I had placed at the end of the shadow-throwing pole had formed part of a wide arc.

When the sunlight slipped away, the Sun Watcher shivered under his robe and complained that his back had begun to ache. We left our shadow-throwing pole where it stood up into the sky and returned to our quarters.

In the morning, after I had made my husband a warm stew for breakfast, I donned my sandals and quickly made my way to the site of the shadow-throwing pole. The gray dog trotted along beside me, for I had been feeding him, and now he held love in his eyes for me. Throughout the morning, I continued to place stones at the end of the shadows cast by the pole until they met the ones I had placed out on the day before. When I had finished, before me lay a smooth, wide arc of stones on the ground.

That afternoon, the Sun Watcher returned with me to show me the next step.

He gazed at the arc and nodded his approval. "From now on, you can do this in one day. Start in the morning and mark the ends of the shadows all throughout the day."

"Yes, I see," I answered.

"Now we will proceed," said the Sun Watcher.

At his direction, I tied a rope to the shadow-throwing pole and stretched it taut. Then I took it around from one side to the other, marking the ends of the half circle that it created with another set of stones. When I had finished, I could see that in two places, the arc made by the sun shadows met the perfect half circle made by the rope.

"The secret," my husband said with smile, "is where the circles cut across each other." He hobbled around to the site of one of those cross marks and looked directly across to the other site. He raised his hand before him and pointed. "This line leads directly to the west," he said as he faced the setting sun. "The other direction is true east."

I stood behind him and gazed over his shoulder.

"With that information, another line can be drawn that runs perfectly north to south. Do you understand?"

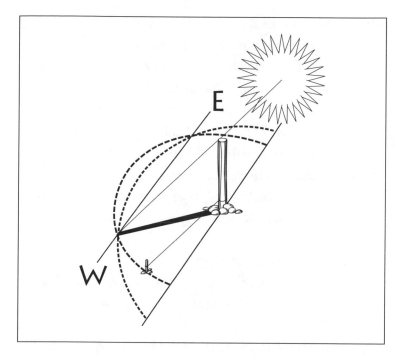

I smiled as I gazed down at those stones upon the ground. It was a simple procedure. "Yes, I do." Something that had seemed so mysterious to me for all of my life was at once so clear.

I looked into his eyes. "Thank you, my husband."

He smiled and put a hand against his back.

"It is time I returned you to our room," I said.

As I walked my husband back up the causeway, I smiled and spoke briefly to friends we met along the way. But I felt changed, for I harbored a knowledge that few others had ever gained. I felt a sense of swelling within my chest, a sensation I had never felt before.

Later that sensation would become very familiar, yet secret within me. And I soon learned to recognize it for what it was. The pride of knowledge. The gift of learning something that one has never known before.

I carried that gift within me as I went down to the low-land villages on the day of the green corn festival. While the corn cooked, I took lessons from my grandmother on how to prepare herb pastes and heated salves that would ease the pain of the joint disease that affected my husband and which had also riddled my grandfather in the later years of his life.

After we had worked together for most of the morning, Grandmother finally turned to me. "I hope he is kind," she said.

I nodded to ease her worries. "He is."

She smiled a toothless grin. "We hear he has taken for you the best of the blue stones brought back from the traders."

"Yes," I answered as I mixed the last batch of paste. But I had almost forgotten about the stones, although they were some of the finest I had ever seen. More green than true blue, they were unusual—deeper and more lustrous than others were. When my husband had set them into my hands, they had felt heavy and warm as though full of the sunlight.

The Sun Watcher had arranged for the finest jewelry maker in all of the villages to make those rare stones into a necklace for me, and I appreciated his efforts to please. But the thing that I longed for was not more jewels, not riches of any kind.

Only knowledge. I longed for more knowledge of the World. And particularly, the knowledge of the sky.

"He has given me more than jewels, Grandmother," I said.

She raised her eyebrows.

But I decided to say no more, to keep the secret that I held only between the two of us, my husband and myself, lest he be thought unfit by the other Priests, lest his decision to share his knowledge with a woman be deemed unwise.

As the festival began, my mother and I dug our teeth into the hot ears of cooked corn and danced and sang songs just as we had in years before, during the green corn days of my youth. My father was among the dancers, and as I watched him, I thought his dancing was the most joyous I had ever seen. Laughter rang out over the sounds of the chanting and singing, and I wished that my husband had felt well enough to journey down into the lowland villages, to share in this celebration.

I searched the crowd for my brother, Jumping Fish, whom I had not yet seen that day. Instead, my eyes fell on another pair of most familiar eyes.

On the other side of the courtyard, pressed in among the crowd, Falcon stood without moving. His eyes were deep and brown as I had well remembered, and as I gazed at him, all the way across the courtyard, I could see that their deep brown circles stilled as he gazed back at me.

The music and the laughter and the chanting seemed to change their sound, growing softer and slower, just as the sound of the wind changes when one turns away from it and it falls no longer upon one's face but against one's back. I stood without moving for long moments, looking into the eyes of the one I loved.

Falcon met my gaze for long moments, and then slowly, he looked over to his side. And there I saw, standing next to him, my friend Red Rope. She did not look at me.

Instead she laughed and clapped her hands together as she watched the dancers twirl upon the hard packed soil of the courtyard. On her face, I saw incredible joy.

I felt rough fingers grasp carefully the skin of my upper arm. Now it was Jumping Fish's kind eyes that I looked up and into. He squeezed my arm and then released it. "They will marry," he finally said. His words told me that which his eyes had already shown me. "Falcon and Red Rope."

I said nothing even though my first reaction was of jealousy, the purest and vilest of all emotions. My grand-mother had once warned me against such feelings, but I did not want to think of Falcon with another. He had promised himself to me, and I had promised myself to him. But as I stood in the courtyard, trying to enjoy the rest of the festival's activities, I willed my feelings to change. I could not have the one whom I loved, yet I wanted his happiness. And Red Rope's, too.

Days later, I tried to make myself thank the Gods. I tried to thank them for their great wisdom and hoped that I would understand their wisdom in years to come. But the truth remained, heavy as a stone in my chest. Two persons whom I loved would build a house in which they would live their lives together. He would farm her family's fields, and she would bear children for her mother's clan. With the help of the Gods, they would find hope and happiness.

I would not have children or a home next to my mother's. But I would gain the knowledge of the skies, and someday I prayed I would understand how I was destined to use it.

10

SEASONS

After the green corn time, preparations began in earnest for the large autumn harvest, the happiest time of the year. A time of much activity when the Gods answered our prayers and rewarded our labors, the harvest time began as the leaves on the corn plants turned yellow-brown and began curling down on the tall stalks. At night, a chill began to sting the air.

In the mornings, I made my husband a hot breakfast and rubbed salve into his limbs and his back. Then I left my home and traveled down to the villages to help with the harvest. I found myself once again, as before, as in the days of my childhood, working alongside my brother Jumping Fish in fields of corn as high as my head. The heavy ears of corn leaned over toward the ground, the bean vines were full of bulging pods, and great shiny yellow squashes lumbered to the ground.

Together, we carried every kernel of corn and every bean and every slippery squash up the trails from our fields to the storage cysts. Again I walked upon the trails used by my People and by my ancestors for many hundreds of years, and my footprints mixed with theirs.

As I worked, I listened to the sounds of insects on leaves, the sweet sounds of songbirds in the trees, the shrieking cries of the hunting birds that flew over the golden fields, and the songs and laughter of my People. I saw my brother's lean brown back before me on the trail, and I felt contentment spread through me like the warmth from a hot fire that sinks down deep into one's skin. Our fields were so full of crops that many trips were needed to complete the harvest and the portage of crops to the village. Corn piled up everywhere, bringing brilliant color to the rooftops of our village houses.

All through the harvest time, the mothers and grandmothers watched for perfect ears of corn to set aside. Those perfect specimens of corn would be saved for ceremonies and more importantly, to be used as Corn Mothers for newborn infants during their presentations to the Sun Father.

The harvest and transportation of crops were arduous tasks, and as the days went on longer and as the Sun rose high in the sky and the heat became stifling, I had to slow my pace. But for me, the cause of my fatigue was not the work at hand, for I was as strong as any of my brothers were, and the sharing of the chores made my heart sing. I grew tired because I knew that after harvest, the first frost would soon come, and then the season to gather pinyon nuts would arrive, and soon after, winter would come again. My husband would need even more of my attention during the long cold winter months ahead, so I knew I must enjoy these days filled with warmth and white light and clear skies for as long as each one of them lasted.

One day, Jumping Fish and I paused to rest and to drink handfuls of water by the river's edge. The gray dog curled into a circle at my feet for a nap. Downriver from where we sat, I could see the meeting place among the willows that once my brother, Falcon, and I had shared, where we had whispered our secrets, where we had made our plans. The Sun had already started to sink low against the horizon, and I watched the lavender light of the sunset settle down over that spot in the willows.

Falcon had gone to live with Red Rope's clan, in a house built by her uncles beside her mother's house. Jumping Fish and I both knew of it, but we did not speak of it. My oldest brother, Shooting Star, had also married and had moved into the house of a girl of the Beaver Clan.

Jumping Fish splashed cool water on his face. "Shooting Star does not wish to remain here, in this village."

I turned to him. "Not in this village?"

"No," Jumping Fish said. "Shooting Star believes we have taken too many trees from our forests. The large animals are migrating away from this area to go further south and north. He has always been happiest while hunting, and therefore, he wishes to follow the animals."

"But what of his wife's family, the rest of the Beaver clan?"

"It seems they desire to journey as well. They hear from the traders a tale of many fertile valleys along a big river to the south and east. They wish to establish villages there, along that great river that we hear of."

I looked down at my hands. I did not want my brother to leave this place. I did not want to be any farther from my family than my marriage had already forced me to be. "And what of our brother, Mockingbird?"

Jumping Fish pondered. "I believe he is in agreement with Shooting Star."

This did not surprise me. My two eldest brothers had always been as close as the Twin War Gods, best friends, just as Jumping Fish and I had been.

"Will he marry, too?"

"I think so," he said as he flashed me a smile. "Although he has not settled on a wife yet."

I found a stone to rest my feet on and let the visions that my brother's words brought to me settle themselves down. "And what of you, Jumping Fish? Have you found one that will make you a good wife? One that will give you a happy life?"

Jumping Fish gazed into the Sun, squinting. "I will not marry."

I laughed at him, for I could remember when I had felt this same way. "Of course you will."

He turned to me. "You misunderstand. I can probably find a wife. But I think I will choose not to."

I puzzled. "But why, my brother?"

He shifted his eyes and let them lay on the spot in the willows where he had once met with Falcon and me, where we had launched our summer adventures. "The spell has been broken. The good medicine. I am afraid it has left us."

I looked closely at my brother's face. "No, not for you," I said.

He continued, "You see, I was as much a part of it as you and Falcon were." He tuned to me. "We were a group of three, don't you see? Just like the three infants born at once to the woman among the Cliff Dwellers. I had dreams for our future, just as the two of you did."

"But you can still find your dream," I urged him.

He sighed. "You have been denied the one you were meant to have." His eyes softened. "I have been just as saddened as you, my sister. So I will take no wife."

I breathed out. "I do not wish you to make such a sacrifice, not for me."

"It is my choice," he said. "I wish always to be free to help you should you need my attention. I do not want ever to be forced to choose between those of my mother's blood and the children born to my wife."

But I did not want to cause my brother a life without a wife, without children. "You would not need to choose," I said. "I do not understand your reason."

"Our mother's clan," he said as he looked back into the Sun. "If you had married in the traditional way, your husband would have come to live within our mother's clan. He would have lived with us. He would have worked in the fields along with us and hunted with us. But it has not come to be. When Mockingbird and Shooting Star marry and join their wife's clans, who will help Father in the fields?"

I let his words sink in.

"Father is not as young and strong as he used to be. He cannot tend the fields alone, without sons to help him."

Finally I answered him. "You are correct. There will be

no other. Not until Summer Wind marries. And that day is many years away."

"So you understand."

"Yes." I looked into his eyes. "It is a choice that shows how generous your heart is, my brother."

He nodded his thanks. Then his shoulder bones relaxed under his skin as if just speaking the words had lifted his burden. The light of the Sun changed to a deeper tone, to the amber color of a fire ember just before the hot center flame dies away.

"My husband has a good heart as well. Do not worry any longer for me."

I could see him swallow back tears.

Over the course of the long winter to come, I often recalled this conversation whenever I wanted to feel a sense of warmth. Whenever I needed to feel the strength of the bond with my own family, I remembered my brother's kindness.

The wisdom of his words, his concern for our father, soon became very clear to me. Like the previous winter, the next winter came down cold from the north. But unlike the previous winter, it came exceedingly dry and windy as if from a cold angry arctic God. Few storms fell down upon us, and little snow covered the ground. Still, the winds blew in icy air from the north, and many of our elders became ill, including our father.

Father lay upon his blankets with a fever for two days and three nights. During one long night, I thought surely he would leave this Earth and go among the Gods, but his strength and the medicine power of the Village Priest saved him. Before the next cold sweep of air came in from the north and west, he could again sit up and take broth from a bowl, and for this, I thanked the Gods.

But even after the fever had passed, Father stayed weakened. He had to remain inside the pithouse for many Moons due to a lingering sickness in his chest, and he became so thin that the skin of his face hung down over his bones, making him look more like a grandfather than a father.

Because of the cold dry air, I kept my husband inside the warm walls of our home for most of the winter. His eyesight worsened over the long months, but he never fell ill. Even with his poor eyesight, he could still feed himself from a bowl, and during his better days, he was able to give me continued sky lessons. Already I held many sky secrets in the deepest chambers of my mind.

One night, the Sun Watcher led me outside on a particularly clear night. We sat with the gray dog curled up at our feet. And on that night, I first began to understand the cycle of the stars. Together we sat on the ledge that faced the Twin War Gods and studied the night sky filled with bright star clusters and hazy swaths of smaller stars.

He pointed upward with a finger. The light on his face was the same pale blue that came out of river ice. "The sky is the home of our Gods, young one," he had said to me. "Sun Gods and Sky Gods, Wind Gods and Rain Gods. There are those who throw thunderbolts and carry the Sun from east to west each day, and those who bring the storms."

"How do you come to know the Sky Gods?"

"By their movement, by their actions," he answered, his breath making a fog that vanished before his next words were spoken. "Study them, young one. And do not anger them. When the Sky Gods are angry, they may punish us with storms, or they may take away what we need, such as the rain."

"How do we please the Gods?" I asked.

"We must pray from our whole heart for everybody, for our People, not just for us but for the whole World that we can have good, healthy lives. The one who takes care of us from above, our Sun Father, will provide for us and will help us to live in a good way. This is what it is to pray, this is what we must pray."

I followed my husband's eyes upward to the skies as I listened. Each word sounded like prayer or music deep in his throat.

"The responsibility of the People is enormous. Ah." He paused as he looked at the sky above. "Such a beautiful World we have been given. The Gods have trusted us to be wise and to work hard, but this is only an experiment, this Fourth World. It cannot be duplicated anywhere else. There is no comparison in the whole plan of the Gods. Look," he said pointing.

My husband stared into the stars. "For many long years, I have studied those tiny specks of light in the blackened sky. I have studied the Sun that brings light and warmth, and the Moon that is moderator between the Earth and the Sun and brings new life to the People."

I saw a black world before me, a deep field dotted with sparkling stars that moved at the slowest of all crawls. Beautiful to be sure, but nothing that I could read, nothing that I could understand.

"If you have patience and study the skies, you will see that new stars rise in the east, just as our Sun does, and the old stars set in the west. You see, young one, we lie at the center of a vast and slowly turning circle of stars. Familiar stars and clusters will return to the sky, always appearing first in the east."

After that, each night after my husband fell into sleep, I came outside and sat on the bench alone. I studied the pattern of stars as they first appeared in the east and traveled above and around our World. Even when the nights grew bitterly cold, I wrapped my feather blanket about me and studied the patterns. I began to memorize their tracks just as I had once memorized the songs of the birds. But later, images of Falcon still flew through my dreams like those stars, like those traveling points of light.

One day, my husband asked me to take him high into the tower on the high mesa to observe the daily sunrise. There the Twin War Gods could not obstruct our view of the horizon. With his one good eye, the Sun watcher studied the exact spot of the sunrise that morning. Although many of the other High Priests shared this knowledge, it was my husband who would name the day in the depths of winter when the time came for the Sun to turn back. And I would stand at his side to see how he did it.

"During the spring and the fall, the Sun changes position on the horizon daily, but when it nears its time to turn back, it slows and barely moves at all." He said this as he shielded his eyes and gazed into the rising, hot yellow Sun. "Look at the landmarks along the horizon. Memorize them."

I looked at the rises and dips along the ridge, at the rocky spikes of mountains that scraped the sky in the east, far away.

"I have looked this way for many years. I know that when the Sun reaches that place, there," he said as he pointed to a sharp dip in the ridge. "And when it greatly slows, it will soon reach its stopping point in the winter. The time for winter solstice, the shortest day of the year, the very middle of the winter."

"Does the Sun stop completely?"

"Yes. For seven days, it rises in the exact same spot on the horizon."

For the next few days, we went to the tower together. In the middle of winter, the Sun rose just south of a very pointed mountain, in a dip in the ridge, and there it remained for days. The Sun Watcher announced to the other Priests that it was now time to turn back the Sun.

Our ceremonies had to begin then, for always a great danger existed. The Sun might stop moving and stay at this winter grave along the horizon, or even worse, the Sun could fall away from the Earth and never return. The ceremonies would ensure that this did not happen.

After the winter solstice ceremonies, the Sun Watcher continued teaching me about the calendar of the horizon. "There, along that ridge," he said. "That is the place where the Sun will rise when it is time to clear the fields, when the Sun is starting to move faster as it travels back to the northern skies."

I followed his finger and formed a picture of the spot inside my head.

"And there," he pointed again. "When the Sun rises there, it is time for squash planting."

Again I made a picture of the place, and I determined

to climb the tower and view the places again and again so that my mind could never forget.

He showed me the exact spot where the Sun would rise on the proper day to begin planting the corn, and the place where the Sun would again stand still on the longest day of summer. There, during summer solstice, the Sun would remain without moving again for seven days before it began its travels back to the south.

Throughout that first winter of my marriage, I tended to my husband's needs and he, in return, shared with me his incredible knowledge that had once belonged only to the Priests. I delighted in my days of studying the sunrise and sunset locations and in my nights of studying the arched patterns of moving stars. Daily I cared for my husband and visited my family, and I found life not unpleasant at all. And when I heard the news that Red Rope would soon give birth to a child, I celebrated. I remembered the lessons from my husband, our need to pray and wish well for all of the People, lest we offend the Gods.

But as winter came to a close, the snows still had not fallen, and the ground was therefore dry and dusty and unfit for planting. I remembered my brother's words and began to fear that something was indeed wrong in the World. Something had been set out of balance. The Rain Maker Priest went into full ceremony in the kivas of the Great House to bring the rains, to please the Rain God, who it seemed was not pleased with us.

But despite his ceremonies, when the Sun reached the point in the sky that announced the time for planting, the soil remained as hard as stone. The much-needed moisture from melted snowfall had given no new life to the land.

The Sun Watcher announced the time for planting; however the rest of the Priests did not know what to do. The fields were as dry as sea salt, and the People were discontent.

"How can we plant the fields when there is no water to nourish the crops?" my father asked when I visited him one day.

I said, "The Rain Dancer Priest is praying day and night, chanting and dancing. He sprays the Earth with sacred cornmeal and shoots arrows at the Sun to bring the rain. He says that the Sky God has spoken to him. The soft spring woman rains will come as soon as we put our faith into the soil, as soon as we plant."

Father shook his head. "Daily more People are coming, moving up to our villages from the villages further south along our river. They are leaving their homes and bringing more mouths that must be fed from our fields."

I put my hand on my father's. "We must believe in the Gods."

"This I have always done, my daughter. But I do not like the signs upon the land. I do not wish to plant when the soil is like sand on rocks."

My father rose to his feet and slowly straightened up. As he hesitantly moved, I could see that he remained frail as a result of his winter illness, that his strength had waned.

He rubbed the lower part of his back. "Already your brother, Shooting Star, wants to follow the big game animals that are leaving this place. Already he wants to go on to new lands in the south."

I lowered my head. "Jumping Fish has told me of this."

Father suddenly looked determined. "I have decided to plant. And I will advise your brother to wait until after the planting time, to see if the spring rains will come and feed the dust-filled fields. This I will do."

So it came to be that on a dry spring day determined by the High Priests, the men planted the fields, carrying out the same intricate ceremonies that had assured good crops for many previous seasons, for many generations. Even though the soil was gray and dusty, they placed their faith in the land and stooped their backs to the ceremonial planting of the first rows of corn.

Four days later, on the day of the major planting, no rain had yet fallen. My father's eyes held worry in those places where men hide their tears. Still, we took our corn seed and gathered in the fields to plant as before. Without the fields we would have nothing to do except hunt for wild game and gather foodstuffs from the forest, else we slaughter our turkeys. We had little choice but to go on, to rely on our faith, to believe in the Priests and their communications with the Gods.

Early in the morning as we began our work, we could see the Moon in the bright blue dome of morning sky. It was a good sign—the Moon showing us her face in the bright daylight of morning. But as we began our planting, something changed.

I worked alongside my mother and dug holes in the dry, cracked Earth. It was harder than it had ever been before to break the soil with our digging sticks, to dig holes one foot deep for corn planting.

My brother, Mockingbird, dug and chopped nearby. All at once, he stopped his work and stared into the sky. "Look," he shouted. "The Sun Father is going away. Something is eating him alive."

I looked up. On the edge of the bright fireball of the Sun, I could see a darkening, as if something were closing down upon the Sun, blocking out its light. I had never seen this before, yet I had heard of it. In years past, this had happened before, but the Priests had managed to save the Sun. Still, it was one of the most frightening of all the tales ever told around the fireside in the winter.

"Stop planting," Father said to all of us. "This is very bad medicine. We must consult the Priests."

We dropped our tools in the field and ran up the trails into the courtyards. Others were doing the same, abandoning their planting and running to the villages. Fear hung in the eyes that I gazed into, a fear of something dark and unknown.

11

THE SKY MONSTER

"What is it, Father?" I asked as we hurried up the trail from the fields. "What is happening to the Sun?"

"This has happened before," he answered me as he walked quickly up the path, his face grim. "It is a monster of the Sky World. We do not know what it is or why it comes. But it is eating our Sun God, and if we cannot make it stop, it will swallow the Sun, and the light of this Earth will go away. The land will become cold and dark, and all the People of the World will perish."

When we reached the courtyard, we found many villagers scurrying about like frightened mice. Women wailed, and dogs barked. The children's eyes blazed with terror as they looked up to observe the slow death of our Sun Father. They stared up at the Sun for as long as their eyes could handle the intense burning light, and they whispered to one another behind their hands.

That light was becoming dimmer as each moment crept by. Slowly, the light of the Sun was fading away. My father and some of the other men went to alert the Village

Priests. Soon we all stood about in a large circle surrounding the Great Kiva and waited for the Priests' response to this unfolding disaster. I worried about the Sun Watcher, my husband. Where was he? Would he be safe? But I knew not what to do, except to wait for help.

As I waited, I occasionally stole a look at the Sun. I had never seen it like this before. No longer round, one side of the burning orb was covered, losing its light. Fear was a large rock in my chest, but I was the wife of a High Priest, and I had to be brave.

I swallowed the foul taste in the back of my mouth. Some of the other woman began falling to their knees, crying and screaming to the Sky Gods to save the Sun. Children began to hide behind their mother's aprons. Some of the dogs began to howl.

Finally, our Village Priests emerged from the Great Kiva wearing their many-colored knee-length sashes and aprons. On their chests hung ornaments of turquoise, shell, and animal teeth. Their bright colors were intended to be gay, to convince the Sun that his children on Earth loved him and did not want him to leave.

One Village Priest carried gourd rattles and sacred cedar sticks in both hands. Others brought forth their sacred prayer sticks topped with kingfisher feathers, their deerskin pouches filled with water-washed stones and their reed flutes.

Our Priests circled the courtyard and began to sing and chant and dance. They signaled for us to join them in prayer. Even the young children were urged to join in the singing and dancing, for it was well known that the Sun Father was fond of children.

Finally, after much dancing in the courtyard, we looked to the sky. The Sun was still slipping away. In a state of excitement, the Priests gathered all of the men that had come running in from their fields. They sent messages for every man from every village to join them in the Great Kiva for this most urgent of all ceremonies. This disaster required the cooperation of all. They needed to make offerings of prayer feathers and sacred corn meal. They needed to chant and pray until they could convince the Swallowing Monster to spit out the Sun and give it back to us.

The women and children had to remain outside the kiva, but we did not cease our efforts. We continued to pray outside the Great Kiva, but it seemed that nothing we were doing was pleasing to the Sky Gods. I was afraid to look up, but when I did, I saw that the Sun was continuing to grow smaller, and the light dimmed as if a heavy fog hung in the air.

Finally, one of the Priests emerged. "We need the Sun Watcher," he called.

Everyone turned to look at me. I had left my husband sleeping in our room within the Great House. Earlier that morning, he had awakened after a fitful night with little sleep. He had taken his breakfast, and then because his bones felt sore, he went back to sleep on his favorite otter fur blanket.

"I will bring him down," I answered. Then I looked for my brother, because I knew I would need help in getting the Sun Watcher down the causeway and to the safety of the villages. But before I could even ask for him, Jumping Fish already stood at my side.

Together, we hurried up the causeway, past the Guard

House that had been left empty in all the excitement and commotion. At the Great House, the High Priests had seen the disaster taking place and had already gathered in one of the kivas for ceremony. I sent a message inside, to my husband. When he emerged, he looked more worried than I had ever seen him before.

I said, "The Village Priests have asked that you join them, with the People, below."

I could hear Jumping Fish's labored breathing as I waited for my husband to answer.

The Sun Watcher looked at me closely with his one good eye. "Yes," he finally said. "I will go with you to the villages."

Jumping Fish and I walked on either side of the Sun Watcher, supporting much of his weight on our shoulders. We took him down the causeway and into the villages, to the Great Kiva. Jumping Fish took him inside the kiva with the other Priests and left me with the women on the outside. I, along with the other women, had nothing else to do but to continue the prayers and glances up toward the waning Sun.

We could hear the throbbing, pounding sounds lifting upward from within, and the deep guttural songs of the ceremonies sung inside the kiva. Normally, we women and children who remained on the outside during such ceremonies could hear nothing. But because their efforts were so strong on this day, we could hear occasional words and phrases and the stomping of many feet on the hardpacked earthen floor within.

After a time as long as a night without sleep, I looked up. I studied the Sun for a few seconds, until I felt its rays threaten to burn the center of my eyes. But I had seen enough, enough to make my heart race with glee. It seemed the Sun was becoming larger again, and I thought I could feel a more intense heat upon my face. "Look," I said to the other women. "It is working."

Mother came to stand beside me. She put a hand on my arm. Slowly as the Sun began to take back its original shape, I felt her relax.

Mother said, "The power of the Priests has never failed us. Again, it has saved us."

Grandmother, leaning heavily on her walking stick, staggered over to us. "I remember a time when I was a young girl," she said. "On that day, the monster completely swallowed the Sun. We were so frightened, because even though it was the middle of the day, the World became as black as a moonless night."

She stopped walking as the light of the returning Sun began to shine on the creased skin of her forehead and her white hair shone like sunlit snow. "And again, it was the medicine power of the Priests that forced the monster to give us back our Sun."

When the Priests began to emerge from the Great Kiva, the women and children shouted and cheered, and many ran about in a frenzy of elation. My husband was the last to emerge, helped by my brother and our Village Priest. As The Sun Watcher came out into the sunshine of the courtyard, everyone began to cheer even louder.

It seemed he would receive the most credit for saving our Sun on that fateful day.

It was a time of joy and celebration as a special feast and continued dancing and praying were planned for that evening. The Sun Watcher stayed with me late into the evening in the village by the ravine, with my People. For the first time, he visited the pithouse where I was born and saw the place where I had lived before I came to him in the Great House. But his eyes revealed no revulsion at the manner in which I had been raised. Instead, he studied my former home with a look of reverence and took his place around the fire with my family.

Later in the evening, we walked alone, back to the Great House. As he limped up the causeway holding onto my arm, he said, "I remember the place where I grew up." His eyes twinkled like a bright star as he spoke. "So long ago," he said. "So long ago."

I remember how soundly he slept that night, and with a smile upon his lips. How pleased he must have been with himself, although he had never said this, even to me. His medicine power had remained great despite his diminishing physical strength. He had saved our villages, had saved us all.

The next morning, as I arrived to help my family continue with the corn planting, I could see that my father had not yet emerged from the pithouse. Even though the morning was already halfway gone, my mother stood outside without my father, waiting with her digging stick and her pouch of corn seeds.

Instead of preparing himself for the planting, Father sat before the morning fire, looking at his hands with his eyebrows drooped over his eyes.

"What is it, Father?" I asked as I lowered myself into the pithouse.

He focused only on the flames. "This is a very bad omen, my child. The Sky Monster coming on the very first day of our large planting." He shook his head from side to side. "I do not like it. And the soil is still so dry. Why cannot the Rain Dancer bring us some moisture for this parched land?"

My father's words and the concern on his face stopped my breathing cold. I did not know how to answer.

"Why is there still no rain? And why did the Sky Monster come to eat the Sun now, during our time of planting? It is bad medicine, my daughter. It is very bad medicine for us."

I put my hand on his, and finally after much quiet talking, I convinced him to join us in the fields and to continue to plant the crops. But in the end, my father's wisdom proved to be true. Before long, it seemed that we could no longer please the Gods, that drought was determined to set in upon us.

12

DROUGHT

I heard through the messages of my brother about the birth of Falcon and Red Rope's child, a boy they named Eagle Claw. The newborn, strong and healthy, was presented to the Sun Father on his twentieth day of life. I could picture the naming ceremony in my mind, although I did not attend it. I had seen it performed many times before, and it was one of my most favorite ceremonies of all.

After twenty days kept in the darkness, the infant would finally be brought out by Red Rope and her mother, and with his perfect ear of corn, his Corn Mother, he would be presented to the Sun Father just as dawn brought first light to the sky. On that day, as the Sun cleared the horizon, Red Rope would lift her son high up in the air, as had been done by all the generations of new mothers, and she would say, "Father, this is your child."

All seemed well on that day, but I could not contain within me the shameful feelings of envy that sometimes swelled like a soreness in my chest. There had been a time when I had believed that Falcon and I, together, would bring children into this World.

I asked my brother about the child. We were standing down by the river, near the place where once the three of us had met and then sought out our adventures. Near that place of childhood gone.

"Is he a handsome child?" I asked as I searched the water for something I didn't know.

"Yes," said Jumping Fish in a low voice, soft with kindness. "He resembles Falcon, and he has large hands with long fingers. He was born with long nails, too, and therefore they chose his first name: Eagle Claw."

I was happy for them. Truly I wished their little family nothing but joy and health, but I also wished I could wash away the heaviness in my heart in the constant flow of the river. I wished it would flood away.

Jumping Fish knew me so well. I caught the look of knowing in his eyes and in his cheeks as they slackened. He said gently, soft as a breeze, "Do you ever wonder, Echo," he said and stopped, lowering his voice even more, "how things would have been different if you hadn't caught the child?"

"It does no good to wonder," I said. "It has been done."

And yet I did wonder, still.

"What if we had never climbed so high?" Jumping Fish continued. "What if we had been standing only a few feet over, in either direction? Just a few feet?"

"I had to save the child. It had been destined, or that is what I tell myself. He simply fell into my hands."

"Why, I wonder?" said Jumping Fish. Then as he watched the river, standing beside me, he seemed to set it free. He shrugged. "You are right, Echo. It does no good to wonder what might have been. It only causes pain."

I let my breath out slowly and prayed for wisdom and for the new child, Eagle Claw, born into Red Rope's clan. "The Sun Watcher says we are all given a bright path to follow. That we must follow that bright path the Gods have decreed for us, lest we fall into darkness."

Jumping Fish shrugged again.

Later we sat by the water's edge and watched the tiny fish that moved together in the shallows as though they were connected by invisible ropes. Barely seen as a collection of silvery stripes with dark dots for eyes, they drifted forward and then surged upward in a current, and finally they jerked in another direction, all as one.

"How do they do that?" I asked.

He shook his head and smiled as he gazed back into the shallows. "I don't know. They are linked by something we cannot see."

Later just for the fun of it, we tried to catch one of those minnows with our hands, but they were too fast and slippery for us. We only wanted to study one closely and then set him free again. But even though we couldn't catch a fish, we splashed and waded and before we knew it, we were smiling and laughing for long moments at a time. It had been a good day, this day I heard of Falcon's son.

But even so, as I walked away from the riverbed, I looked upstream to the place that had been our former childhood meeting place, that spot in the willows, and it seemed far, far away now. I could still see the place, but I knew in one instant that our childhoods were now over, washed away as though on the rippling waves of the river.

Even the bright stars of memory that visited me at night were beginning to fade. It seemed that all had changed and so quickly, just as everything seemed to be changing for our People, too.

Indeed, it was the last day of joy for many more Moon seasons afterward.

Although our People had finished planting the fields, although we had followed our faith despite the appearance and defeat of the Sun Swallowing Monster, the soft spring rains did not come. We had to begin carrying water from the river in our water jars and pouring the water onto the cracking soil of the fields. But we could not carry enough water to make up for the lack of rain. The only corn plants that sprouted that year were the ones that grew on lowlands near the water's edge, and even those plants grew only half as tall as they had in years before.

Some of the squash and bean plants sprouted and ran along the ground, but upon the arrival of summer heat, they began to curl and dry and turn brown.

It seemed the Rain Gods had abandoned us. Sometimes, from the top of the mesa, I could see the storms pass somewhere away from us, against the horizon. Sometimes so close I could hear the birds chattering about it in the trees, and I could smell water in the wind that blew against my face. I could taste the sweet rain upon my tongue as I breathed in the air. Still the storms avoided us, and only a few drops of water fell on our fields. And the corn that did survive the drought was not of the quality that we had grown to expect.

Finally in late summer, a storm came our way. But it was an angry man-rain, the angriest heavy man-rain I had ever seen. It came down so hard it damaged the remaining bean and squash plants. It tore the leaves on the squash plants and flattened the bean vines against the ground. The Earth was so parched by this time that most of the rainwater simply ran off the ground without soaking into it, as though it had landed on stone instead of soil.

During the time when we should have begun our fall harvest, each family had to start going into their storerooms for food. The men went away on large organized hunting expeditions, but they returned discouraged.

"Many of the streams have dried up," Jumping Fish told me after he returned from the hunt. "The lack of rainfall has affected everything, especially the plants, and therefore the animals."

I asked him, "What were you able to find?"

"Only the prairie dogs, grouse, and rabbits are easy to find. Finally, after we traveled many days to the north, we came upon a small herd of deer. However, we killed only two of them, and the rest escaped into the high country where we could not follow." He took a deep breath. "It seems that our brother Shooting Star was correct. I think the animals are leaving this area, following the water."

"What will Shooting Star do?"

Again my brother breathed in deeply before he said the words. "He will leave this place with his wife and her clan. They will be gone before winter comes to the land."

I looked down at the dust on my sandals. I knew where he would go. I was the one to say it. "He will go south and east to find the big river."

Jumping Fish nodded to confirm my conclusion, and his eyes were hazy with sadness.

Every day I began to hear of other clans leaving. I heard of villages downriver from us that were almost empty, the only villagers remaining behind those too old or ill to travel. I heard that People in the Center of the World had begun to leave that place, too. That fine city of many great houses much larger than our own was beginning to empty out as well. And always, it seemed the journeyers sought to find the big river in the south and the east, a river so large, the travelers had told us, that it never ran dry.

"And Mockingbird will go with him," I said.

"No," Jumping Fish said, startling me with his answer. "His concern for our father will keep him here, at least for now."

I had seen my father earlier in the morning and understood the reason for our brother's concern. Ever since the Sun Swallowing Monster had appeared in the sky the spring before, Father had not been the same. And after the crop failure, his spirits sank even lower. Often he sat before the fire staring into the flames as though looking for some answers there. And often when he spoke, he complained about the lack of the rain and the ineffectiveness of the Rain Dancer Priest.

Once I had said to him, "Father, it does no good to sit before the fire."

He said, "It does no good to do anything. We have angered the Gods. They will continue our punishment for a long time."

I didn't know what to say.

"The only thing that brings me happiness is that you will not be harmed. You live in the Great House. You will not go hungry."

He was not alone in his feelings. For all of the summer and throughout the time when we should have been harvesting our crops, the People had paced the ground and expressed their discontent about everything. We had experienced our first total failure of crops. The People focused their anger against the Priests, and particularly the Rain Maker Priest, the husband of my friend, Corn Tassel, because he had failed to bring the moisture the crops needed.

Corn Tassel followed me outside one night shortly after the hunting party had returned, after they had divided the meager kill among the clans, after they had given a share to the High Priests. When the Hunting Chief turned over the High Priests' share of the meat, I had been standing outside the Great House and saw it happen. The look I saw on the face of the Hunting Chief, a man who had been my father's friend for many years, a man I had always known to be a good and fair man, frightened me. I could scarcely believe the anger I saw burning beneath the surface of his skin. He handed over the meat and lowered his eyes, but I could see the tightness in the skin that spread over his jaw and the hardness in his eyes.

"I am frightened," Corn Tassel said that night. We sat together on the ledge where I often sat and studied the night sky.

I nodded my understanding, as I did not want to give my friend false assurances, especially after what I had witnessed in the face of my father's friend earlier that day. "The rains must come soon," I said. "The People must be given reason to hope."

Corn Tassel swallowed so loud I heard her. "My husband has been trying all the ceremonies that have always worked before. He dances and chants until his voice almost leaves him."

"I have heard him outside the kivas."

"I have to make him a warm broth to soothe the back of his throat, and even so, when he speaks, I can barely hear him. He speaks only in a whisper, like the wind sighing in the tops of the trees. And he has worn blisters on his feet from so much dancing."

I turned to her. "Soon the Gods will hear him."

Corn Tassel took my hand. "But the People. They are angry, aren't they? They blame him, don't they?"

I looked into her eyes. "Some of them do, yes. It seems they were unhappy about giving us a share of the meat from the hunting expedition."

Her eyebrows flew upward. "Do you think they might stop paying the Priests their tribute?"

"Let us not worry. We still have plenty of food in storage."

But the worry would not leave my friend's eyes. "My husband is not a hunter," she said. I could see the thoughts traveling over her face as she spoke. "I have a child to feed."

I thought of her only child. Little Moon was now a large and plump, laughing boy who regularly played with his miniature bow and arrows and chased the gray dog around in circles on the top of the mesa.

Two days later, the Rain Dancer and Corn Tassel disappeared, carrying with them their child and a portion of the stored food from our storeroom. She had never spoken to anyone about their plans, nor had the Rain Dancer told any of the other High Priests. I was sure that if she had told anyone, it would have been me, and because she didn't speak of it, I knew that their fear of discovery must have been great. When I heard of their disappearance, I looked up at the sky, at the Gods who lived overhead, and I said a silent prayer for their safety.

A few days after that, my brother Shooting Star left with his wife's family, of the Beaver Clan, some of the Village Priests, and other members of the Clan. They left early in the morning after saying goodbye to all who had gathered in the courtyard to see them off on their journey. With them they carried only a favorite piece of pottery and a water jar, some clothing, weapons, and dried foodstuff in pouches. They would not carry items that could easily be made again in their new homes, for they had many long valleys and mesas to travel over to reach their destination.

When I said goodbye to my brother, I could not feel sadness because his face was so full of joy. He was going off into the unknown, something he had always loved to do, and his expert hunting skills would sustain them along the way. The Gods had destined him for this journey, and I could not question the wishes of the Gods. But every time I thought of the days to come without my brother's face in them, it ached in my ribs.

And as I turned away to return to the Great House, I heard a man whisper to the man who stood next to him, "Now there will be less mouths to feed."

That night as I sat outside on my ledge facing the Twin War Gods, alone without my friend, Corn Tassel, I wondered what other bad things could the winter bring after such a bad growing and harvest time. The Sun set against my back as I sat in my spot on the high mesa, and as the light began to slip away from the sky, I noticed something as I watched, something I had never noticed before.

As the light slowly receded away around me, I saw that the darkness of nightfall came not from the sky, but instead from the Earth, rising up from the ground. The darkness began on the Earth, where we stood and ate and planted and lived.

This was a dark time that would require new ways of doing things, new ideas. Already one had occurred to me. Instead of looking to the sky as the source of our problems, perhaps we needed to look at the soil for answers.

13

THE RAID

Before the onset of the deep winter, another large band of villagers left for the land to the south, among them some of my aunts and uncles and cousins of the Waterfall Clan. From the mesa top, outside the Great House, far below me I could see the band of travelers in a long dark line, black spots like ants against the recent frost, weaving their way down the river road amidst the crystal fog of their breaths.

Throughout the winter, those of us left behind ate from the storerooms, from remnants of the good harvests that now seemed so long ago. Daily we prayed our gratitude that the elders had taught us so well, that during those good years, we had put away the extra corn and beans and dried meat that would now have to sustain us until the next harvest. Daily the wives of the High Priests went to the cairn of rocks piled at the base of our Twin War Gods to pray and to make offerings of miniature bows and arrows and prayer plumes.

"Next year," my husband said to me. "Next year the

crop will be a good one. We will refill our storerooms, and those who left will be sorry."

I didn't want those who had left, especially my brother Shooting Star, to be sorry. But I did hope for their eventual return. And because my husband made his predictions with such conviction, I believed him.

Late in the winter, on a day bright with sunshine, a day that held the promise of a warm spring to come, I saw tiny shadows moving up the river road, coming in the direction of the large villages below the mesa. I grew curious as to whom the visitors could be, for it was early for any traders to be calling. But the Sun Watcher had not yet eaten his morning stew, and so after fetching the water, I returned to our rooms to cook and care for him.

Later I would hear the cries and screams of my People from below the mesa top, and I would grow to regret that I had assumed all visitors were friendly. I raced down the narrow rock causeway upon hearing the cries, but by the time I had reached the village by the ravine, my family's village, it was all over. Ruthless nomads who did not work to grow their own food, who lived instead by stealing the food of others, had robbed us.

In our village, I found Jumping Fish standing with his hands helpless at his sides. He was standing over my brother Mockingbird.

"The nomads came to rob us of our food stores," he said, choking on tears. "They hit him with a large club made of heaviest wood when he tried to stop them." He looked down at my brother, and I followed his eyes. I managed to take one breath, only one, before my grief began to cry out from inside me.

I wailed while Mother and I bathed my brother's body and washed his hair. We folded his arms across his chest and tied them together to hold them in place as we wept and prayed. We folded his legs up tightly to his body the same way they had once been positioned when he was an infant in the womb. Then we wrapped him in a soft cotton blanket, a large feather blanket, and finally with matting.

We could not bury him in the ground because it was frozen, hard as solid stone. Instead we had to bury him in the great trash pile below the mesa. After Jumping Fish and I dug out the grave, we placed water and strips of dried meat in the hole so that our brother would not go hungry on his journey to the Otherworld. We also laid his favorite bow, arrowheads, and a digging stick in the grave beside him. We made a mask of cotton to cover his face so that the Cloud People would recognize him when he entered their World. After we filled the grave with dirt and stones, we returned to the village to purify ourselves by washing our hair and by fumigating our clothing in smoke.

Jumping Fish shook his head slowly from side to side, and the size of his grief seemed to swell in the air around him. "Mockingbird should have left with our brother Shooting Star. He should have abandoned this place."

"Don't say that, brother. He is happy now. Our brother is with the Gods."

"He should not be," said Jumping Fish. "We have lost so much, and now more."

Already our father was in despair, and now Jumping Fish was losing his faith, too. Someone had to stay faithful. I had to remain believing in good. "The Sun Watcher tells me that next year we will have a bountiful harvest."

But Jumping Fish simply looked at me with tears in his eyes and said nothing.

Although I did not wish to hear it, later I heard the retelling of the raid in many ways. The warlike nomads had descended upon us silently, without warning. At first all had assumed as I had, that they were friendly visitors. But as soon as the villagers realized the nomads had come to steal our food, the men ran to protect their families and their storerooms. The nomads drew out clubs and sticks to use as weapons, and our men, who were not accustomed to fighting, could not hold them off. They were no match for the nomads who fought without mercy, killing many of our young men, among them Mockingbird, who sought to stop them.

For four days Mockingbird's spirit remained in his body. Each day, I went to the gravesite to place my food and water upon the Earth that covered his body. And each day before I left, I turned to the Twin War Gods that towered over us all, asking the questions that were now beginning to clutch me during the long hours when I should have been sleeping. Why had they failed to protect us? Why had they not turned our adversaries into stone, as they had promised the People who lived in their shadows over many generations?

At sunrise on the fourth morning, the spirit of Mockingbird left our World, venturing back into the Mother Earth through the sipapu, the ceremonial floor opening that led to the Spirit World, through which he would find his way. After this day, we were not to speak of Mockingbird again, or even to think of him, so that our grief would not cause us to become ill.

But Father could not forget. He seemed not destined to regain his health from his previous winter's illness, and after the shock of losing one of his sons, he seemed not to have the will to try to heal himself from within. He grew weaker even after spring finally came to the land. Therefore, Jumping Fish was the only one left to hunt for fresh game for our family. Jumping Fish, Mother, and I were the only ones left to plant the fields. Again, we planted in dry, dead soil, praying that this season, the Gods would hear our pleas and send rain. We hoped, but between us we shared darting, fearful eyes.

We desperately needed to have a good growing season. During the raid, the nomads had killed many of our best hunters, and because much of the stored food had been taken, our food stores were left dangerously low. All of the tastier food had soon been consumed. Pinyon nuts, dried fruits, roots, squash, and dried berries were completely depleted. Now every meal consisted of meat, corn mush, and beans.

"Is there nothing new?" my husband asked me one evening after I helped him with his bowl of stewed meat.

"No," I answered. "We have only what is left in the backs of our storerooms."

"Ah," he said and rocked his head once. "These are dangerous times."

"But why?" I asked him. "Why must we go through dangerous times?"

He smiled. "I cannot sit and talk with the Gods as I talk to you, my young one, my young wife. But I can venture a guess."

"What?"

He pursed his lips. "I surmise that this is a test, a test of our faith. We are intended to pray more, to give more, to do without more."

"I don't understand."

Now his face was still, serious. "Perhaps we are not meant to understand everything."

But I had thought the High Priests did just that.

Again to our despair, our prayers were not answered. After a few hopeful spring rains fell on the new crops, the drought returned, and from the first day of summer until the last, no more rain fell from the sky. We met the dry air and scorched Earth each day with either confusion or anger. I did not show my fear, for I was the wife of a High Priest, but it was beginning to live inside me, too, like an illness. I tried to move about unnoticed again, just as once I had done when I wanted to sneak away.

Soon the shallower sections of the river dried up, and fish floundered until they died in the mud along the shores, bringing the stench of death to the wind-blown dust. The corn plants yellowed, withered, and curled down to the ground. We could not carry enough water from the river to keep them alive. But still we waited because any day, the rains could come. Any day.

For two more years, however, it was not to be. Sometimes the skies teased us with occasional rains that ran quickly away like snakes off the dry, dusty ground. And when the big rains finally did come, they were angry, hard, man-rains that beat into pulp whatever small garden plants we had managed to grow. In the winters, more and more of our very young and very old villagers became ill, and other small parties of travelers began to leave the land of the Sky Watchers. Fear caused our People's normally loving hearts to turn as cold as stone. Distrust toward the High Priests became openly expressed, and as our situation worsened, I grew reluctant to take the Sun Watcher beyond the walls of the Great House that kept him warm.

In the middle of the following summer, as the Sun blazed high in a pale blue sky, Jumping Fish took me away with him, as far north as we could travel in one day, just as we had often done before in the days of our youth.

"Every day the anger of our People toward the High Priests grows stronger, Echo," he said that day as we waited in an old bear wallow in a spot of shade. "You must be able to care for yourself, to hunt for food."

For the first time, I let my despair show. "What has happened to us, my brother?"

Jumping Fish sighed. "Perhaps the Gods are letting us know their wishes. Perhaps they wish us to leave this place and begin again in new lands. Perhaps we are to farm new fields and drink fresh waters."

I gulped. "It is true that the villages no longer hold the songs of happiness, only the songs of sorrow. Many days the stench of death surrounds us."

"Someday soon I must take Father away from this place." He looked into my eyes. "Every day his spirit grows weaker, his and those of many other fathers and uncles. Already he and the others of our secret kiva society are teaching me the legends, the rituals, and the chants so that I can conduct our ceremonies without them." Jumping Fish looked at me with pain in his eyes. "I think they have foreseen their own deaths. They want to make sure that the stories and secrets are passed on before they die."

I knew what he meant—the stench of death was everywhere—where once we had smelled flowers and tall sleepy grass. And always the dull light of fear dimmed our People's eyes and made them wary. I said, "Do not speak of it."

"We must speak of it, don't you see?" My brother's face had changed into that of a man's, filled with the worries of older men.

I lowered my eyes and nodded.

He continued, "While Father and Grandmother are still well enough to travel, I must go. I must take them away to the south to find our brother, Shooting Star."

I nodded my understanding. "Of course. Father needs to see his son happy and thriving. Here Father will always remember Mockingbird."

"Sh-h-h. Do not speak of him, Echo. Let him live happily among the soft clouds that float in the sky." Jumping Fish let out a long breath, and then he turned to me. "You must learn to hunt. I do not know what comes with the sunrises of future days. You must learn to hunt, so that you will never go hungry."

Over the next days, Jumping Fish taught me as many skills in hunting as he could fit into daylight's time. He taught me how to lay traps for smaller game. Then he taught me how to find the larger game, how to seek out their watering holes, how to stalk them and run them down, how to handle a bow and arrow, how to shoot and kill.

The days were long and hot and bright like a polished bowl, and even though we had hunting to do, my brother and I found moments for smiling. Once we sat in the shade of a great, old, grandfather cottonwood, and we found the tiny red and black insects that crawled over our hands and

fingers. Another time we ran across an open meadow just
for the sheer freedom of it.

I took easily to the bow and arrow, for I had watched
my brothers with envy for many years, studying their
movements. But the spear thrower proved more difficult
for me to master.

"You must learn this. You must." Our moments of fun
were over. I'd never heard such desperation in my brother's
voice. "Think of it as a way to lengthen your arm, Echo,"
Jumping Fish instructed me. He took the long flat piece of

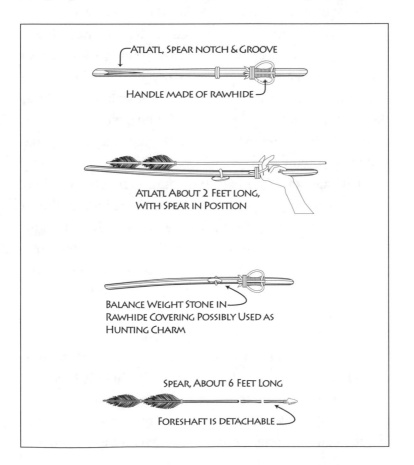

ATLATL, SPEAR NOTCH & GROOVE

HANDLE MADE OF RAWHIDE

ATLATL ABOUT 2 FEET LONG,
WITH SPEAR IN POSITION

BALANCE WEIGHT STONE IN
RAWHIDE COVERING POSSIBLY USED AS
HUNTING CHARM

SPEAR, ABOUT 6 FEET LONG

FORESHAFT IS DETACHABLE

polished wood and placed a dart in the groove that ran down the middle of the spear thrower. He crooked his forefinger and middle finger in the rawhide loops that hung on either side of the spear thrower, and then he held his hand up near his shoulder, with his palm opened and his fingers turned back toward his shoulder.

Jumping Fish ejected the dart by jerking his hand forward. "With good use of a spear thrower," he told me, "the dart travels farther, straighter, and lands harder than if it is thrown by hand."

That summer, I practiced with the spear thrower until I could hit the trunks of trees, dead in their centers. Every day that I did not feel like practicing, when my legs ached from all of my other labors in my husband's room, I remembered the desperation in my brother's voice. And by the time summer had ended, I had managed to take down a doe with the spear thrower, and managed to trap a large badger, all on my own.

I stalked game and set traps and practiced my skills with the spear thrower all during the daylight, and then I ran home to cook and care for the Sun Watcher at night. Often as we sat before the fire in the chill evening air, I looked to my husband for any sign that he might give me, any sign of hope. But if he had experienced any visions of what lay ahead for our People, he no longer shared them with me, and it was not a wife's place to prod.

It was not until after one more winter had passed, when his vision had left him completely, that my husband decided to speak of it. In the spring he had sent me to read the signs along the horizon and to announce the correct day to begin planting. Another spring planting season had begun, another season during which we planted the last of our corn seed, this time again in dry, dead soil. Then he began to speak to me of other things.

"There is one secret of the skies I have yet to share with you."

I looked up, startled that he had kept any bit of his knowledge from me. He had always been so open, just as long ago he had promised me. "What is it?"

"A Stand Still Moon. It is coming our way again."

A strange feeling, like clear river water, ran through my chest. "How do you know this? How do you know this to be true?"

He smiled. "Remember that I am an old man of many years. I can recall other Stand Still Moons, others that came before the one that arrived in the year of your birth. I have noticed that it happens regularly, in a cycle, as in the cycles of the stars. Once in every eighteen years, it will happen. Then for almost two years, the full Moon will rise between the Twin War Gods."

"Are you certain of this?" I asked him.

"You are nearing your eighteenth winter, are you not?"

"Yes."

"Then soon we will again be blessed by a Stand Still Moon. The Moon will reach a high northern point so that once again, the full Moon will rise between the Twin War Gods as we see it at the Great House. I believe that with the return of the Stand Still Moon, all the riches and gifts of days past will return to the People."

"How is this true, yet no one has spoken of it?"

"The High Priests share this knowledge with me. We have always known the season of the Stand Still Moon to be a time of special gifts, and therefore we planned our building times accordingly, so as to receive its blessings. Most of the Great House and its additions were built during seasons of the Stand Still Moon."

"Why, then, have you not told all of the People?"

"It is best to wait until the right time to reveal such things. But as clearly as I know the night skies, I know that a Stand Still Moon is coming."

I felt that river of hope surge upward within my chest. A Stand Still Moon. A Stand Still Moon had not appeared between the two rock pinnacles since the year of my birth, yet another one would appear soon. Surely this was a time for rejoicing. Surely this would bring the dark days to an end.

"May I tell the others?'

He pondered. "Do you think it wise to do so?"

"The People need some reason for hope. Otherwise more will leave this place. Already the Center of the World is all but abandoned, home now only to the whistling wind, or so the few poor traders that still come here have said. The Cliff Dwellers in the west have come down out of their homes and left their great houses to ruin. They, too, are traveling away from this land."

"It is the most treacherous time for our People, when hope and faith fail. Yes," the Sun Watcher said, "tell all of the People who remain here that their faith will be rewarded. The Stand Still Moon is coming soon, and with it, prosperity will return to this land."

14

SEASON OF HOPE

Throughout the planting season, the news I spread among those clans still remaining in our villages brought joy and above all else, hope. A sense that, for reasons we did not yet understand, the Gods had put us through this test of our faith. They had tested us with drought and with the raiding of our foodstores by nomads. We had endured the killing of our young men, the failure of our crops, and much illness and death.

But soon, those of us who remained in this place, our home, would be rewarded by the blessings of the Stand Still Moon. Each day the People whispered about them behind their hands, and each night, they waited for and prayed for them. It was a better time for us who lived in the Great House because some of the anger against us had dissipated. We had restored hope.

In the Great Kiva, the great circular chamber that recreated the dome of sky above, the largest of all ceremonies in our history was held. All the remaining Priests joined together and day after day, they chanted and prayed. All of the men from the mesa villages, from the river villages, and from villages in the hills that surrounded us came to join them also, joining together their strength in the fight against drought and enemies.

The endless ceremonies proved difficult for the Sun Watcher. Each night it became more and more exhausting for him, and often I had trouble getting him to make the climb back to the Great House at night. Even though he leaned on me for support, it seemed that his limbs were draining of their remaining strength. Still, he attended each ceremony well into the night, and when afterwards, we returned to our rooms, I fed him with my fingers and helped him to drink from our bowl. I rubbed the healing salve into his joints and put him to bed under many blankets of warm turkey feathers.

Early in the spring, just after planting season, the rains came softly with the sound of a gentle beating on a worn old drum. The water smelled of sky, and it soaked into the ground and sent the corn stalks growing like weeds out of the brown soil and shooting straight for many Cloud People. Bean vines began to snake across the ground, and squash leaves rolled out of their stems.

Although fewer fields had been planted to conserve the remaining seed corn, fewer mouths remained to be fed. With a successful harvest, we would have enough for all to eat heartily again, to hold our ceremonies and dances. We would have reason again to celebrate.

"It is happening," I told my husband one day. "It is raining. Would you like me to take you outside to feel the rain on your skin?"

He smiled. "No, young one. You must go out and dance if you like. Then come back and tell me of it."

The men spent every spare minute watching over our fields, for it had been many years since we had been so blessed with growing crops. Jumping Fish and our cousins tended to the Waterfall Clan fields, inspecting each row of corn, every bean and squash plant. Not one insect would be allowed to feast on a single leaf. Not one weed would be allowed to twist itself around the stems and stalks of our plants.

Mother and Grandmother stayed close to the pit-house, caring for Father and cooking the remaining food from the storeroom. They would make no pottery this year. No repairing or building of homes would be done either, for the elders were afraid for us to use the water to make mortar. The river still ran much lower than it had in the good years past. It was still trying to recover from many years of drought.

I practiced my hunting skills and took to the open spaces as often as I could. I also gathered yucca leaves and juniper root bark to use to make new baskets. I found flowers blooming and fruits ripening and took those that could be used and saved for dyes back to my mother. Together Mother and Grandmother and I sang the Song of the Basketmaker as we worked together outside the pithouse that was once my home.

"The season for rebirth is upon us," I told them as we worked.

My mother's eyes held hope but also reservation. "We will see," she said. But I did not worry as much as I had before. Father's sadness and worries had simply begun to infect her. But with a good harvest, they would see. We would stay in our World. And it would feed us again. It would take care of us just as it had for generations.

But I found that it was impossible to see into the blank face of the future. I had no foresight as to what was to come. And for the first time I started to believe that no one else, not even the High Priests, did either.

On a warm windy day in the middle of the summer, I took to the hills north of the mesa to set traps for small game. Instead of returning to the Great House, I decided to take to the high country again, as I had done so often in the days of my childhood. I found the steep canyon that once I had climbed with my brother and Falcon, on the day of the green corn festival. I remembered climbing the canyon and then, sitting on top of the mesa, arguing with Falcon and Jumping Fish. I remembered how I had fallen on the way back down and how I had tried to hide my cuts.

I let those memories wash over me as I gazed up the steep canyon trail. At once, I knew I must return to the top of that mesa, to look back over the scene I had once shared with my childhood companions. I grabbed a branch to brace myself and began my ascent.

To my surprise, I made the climb easily, with more agility than I had remembered having when I was still a young girl. On top, I could see everything as clearly as I had once seen it before, the Great House on top of the triangular mesa, the Guard House, the ridgeline leading down to the villages below. The memories of that day, so many years earlier, brought great happiness back into the center of my heart. I sat on the same stone I had once shared with Falcon and Jumping Fish and let the afternoon soar by as if on wings.

But on this day, even though I could remember those days of my childhood, I looked at our homeland with different eyes. I looked with the eyes of one who had become a woman, with the eyes of one who clearly understood the worries of our elders and the cycles of change that the years would somehow teach us to endure. I looked with the eyes of a young woman who would not become a mother because I had married a kind but elderly man too old and sick to father children. Only gentle touches had passed between us. I would have to settle for the Great House and the gift of knowledge instead.

I saw something in the distance. It looked like a cloud of black smoke. Far away, over the river bottoms, it rose and bloomed, and then, caught by the wind, it swept over the villages far below me. I watched for only a moment longer before I jumped to my feet and ran for the canyon. Running as fast as I could, I held my breath deep within my chest, and I prayed. Please don't let it be. Please don't let it be a fire in our fields.

I lowered myself down the steep canyon as fast as I dared, and then I raced through the meadow that separated me from the village. Now I could see it clearly ahead of me. Hot orange flames lit up the ground, and smoke filled the air I would run into. Soon I could smell and taste the burning ash in my nostrils and on my tongue. The villages were burning; the fields were burning, too. I jumped the stream and ran until I met face to face the dense black smoke blown my way from the villages.

I covered my mouth and nose with my apron, and coughing, I ran first to the fields for it was there where I knew I would find the most People, where I knew I must help. Our homes could be rebuilt one day, but our fields this season could not be replaced. They must not be destroyed. I found a line of men, women, and children all carrying the largest water jars they could manage, dragging them in from the river, and dousing the water on the burning fields.

Others took skins and branches and tried to beat out the smaller flames that ran along the ground and spread out from one plant to another like runners. Another line of men was at work digging a trench in the ground to keep the fire from spreading to fields not already burning. I grabbed a digging stick and started to help the men with the trench, all the while my eyes burning with such intensity that I often had to close them. Tears ran down my cheeks, and I coughed violently as I worked. For a moment I thought surely I would choke on the smoke-filled air. The fire's heat laid its claim to my chest and robbed me of my ability to breathe.

Still I worked as hard as I could until the wind picked up, and sparks blew into our faces. Sparks took hold of the long strands of my hair. I dropped the digging stick and pounded away at the long strands with my hands. Pain pricked my palms, but I ignored it as I rid myself of the sparks and reached for my digging stick again.

But just then, a man of the Owl Clan called for us to retreat, to pull back, lest we burn to our deaths. We turned and, coughing and gasping for air, we left the trench we had been digging and stood by with our hands helpless at our sides as wind-blown sparks caught fire in our beautiful tall corn plants and began to burn them to the ground. Tears ran down my blackened cheeks as I watched. But the men only stood, silently watching their promising season's work burn, and then blow away in soot and ash.

"All is lost," I heard one man mumble.

I later learned that the fires had been set by yet another band of hungry nomads, who had set out to steal from our food stores. This time they entered the pithouses as well, searching for food. They clubbed to death some of the men who had tried to defend their homes, as they had clubbed my brother Mockingbird. In the fighting that ensued, the nomads set fire to the thatched roofs of the pithouses, and carrying torches, they fled through the fields, setting them on fire as well.

It was not until the following day that we learned the extent of the damage in both lives and in crops lost. All but one field and a small part of another had burned. Many pithouses had burned down to the stone bedrock upon which they sat, and all but a few of the storerooms had been emptied. Three men had lost their lives, and in the most tragic of all events, a woman had been trapped alone in her pithouse as her roof caught fire and burned her to her death. That woman, I learned later, was my old friend, Red Rope.

15

MESSAGE FROM THE SUN

I did not go with Red Rope's clan to bury her, for I was not asked and did not wish to intrude. But instead I wailed my most beautiful song of mourning in the voice that once had been praised. I could do no more. It was the best gift I had to give.

And although I would tell no one, I sang for Falcon on that night, too. I sang for Falcon, who had lost a wife and for his young son, who had lost a mother. And then I cried for us all, for all of the People who had learned to live with sorrow.

Four days later, after we had mourned the dead, the men began to construct tall lookout towers so that someone could always watch for enemy intruders. We dared to use water from the river to make mortar, knowing that we could not withstand another attack upon our People and our storerooms. In the Great Kiva, the men gathered together to make shields and war sticks and other weapons of war. But we were not warriors; we were farmers. In my heart, I knew they could not win a face-to-face battle with the warrior nomads. But it was something the men felt they had to do.

During the same Moon as the fire, I was awakened one morning by excited voices outside our room of the Great House. I didn't know what was happening, but I had learned to live with dread, even in my sleep. I looked to my husband and saw that the Sun Watcher still slept soundly. I dressed quickly and slipped up through the doorway above. Outside I found all of the other High Priests standing along a high wall of the Great House. Staring into the rising Sun of that morning, they talked excitedly among themselves.

I approached Pond Lily, a High Priest's wife who had become my friend since Corn Tassel had left. Often we walked for water together and shared songs, and there had even been some moments when we forgot about the fires and the fields that now lay in ruin. Many days we had acted happy even when we didn't feel happy. Sometimes I thought that all the sorrow and worry had brought only more sorrow and worry. Perhaps we needed to trick the Gods into believing we were happy, so that more happiness would come our way.

Pond Lily was very heavy with child, and as she stood on the wide wall of the Great House, she looked frightened. The look on her face alarmed me, for I knew her to be a brave woman. "Our Father, the Sun, has been marked with dark spots. Look!" she cried as she pointed.

I shielded my eyes and looked at the fiery ball of the Sun Father as he rose up over the eastern plains. The bright light and its heat upon my eyes were almost too much to bear, but just as I turned my eyes away from it, just then, I, too, saw the spots. On the face of our Sun Father, spots had grown in patches just as a disease sometimes grows on the backsides of leaves. Several dark spots of varying sizes could be seen.

Not another bad omen! I did not know how the People could endure it.

Quickly I ran back along the wall to the room I shared with the Sun Watcher. I scrambled down the ladder and wondered, what of Pond Lily's and my happy tricks? Had they only angered the Gods more?

My husband awakened as I drew near. Then I whispered, "Husband, wake yourself. The Sun, our Sun Father, has become diseased. His face is covered with black spots none of us has ever seen before."

The Sun Watcher's face remained sleepy, without moving. Slowly he lifted himself to one elbow. "Tell me, Echo. Are the spots large in size?"

"Some of them are. Yes."

The Sun Watcher let out a long, slow breath.

"What does it mean?"

Finally he answered, "I have seen such spots before, and I can tell you that they come and go. Most People fear them, but just as we sometimes get sores on our skin, so does the Sun Father."

"Many times the sores on our skin heal."

"Yes," he said. "And that is what I believe will happen to the spots on the Sun Father. They, too, will heal with the coming of the Stand Still Moon."

I jumped to my feet. "Shall I tell the People? Shall I tell them not to worry?"

He looked so tired and old. For the first time in many Moons I saw how frail my husband had become, how listless. "This decision is yours now, young one," he said with effort, and slowly he lay back into his blankets.

Throughout the rest of the day, I spread the news as fast as I could, roaming about from one village to another. As I went around, I found that some of the villagers were already preparing to leave.

"Because of the fire, we will not have enough food," one man told me. "And now it seems the Sun Father is sick, too. We must leave at once for other lands."

"But the Stand Still Moon. The Stand Still Moon is coming," I answered him. "Do not leave in fear. The Sun Watcher has told me—"

"The Sun Watcher?" The man looked at me with a face like clay that has hardened in the sunlight. "The High Priests have done nothing to help the People during these troubling times. Do not speak to me about the Sun Watcher."

I stood motionless as he walked away. Shielded most of the time in the Great House, I had not realized how irate the People were until that moment. I did not recognize the depth of the anger held by my People toward the High Priests.

Then I remembered the days of my childhood, when I, too, did not like the High Priests. I remembered the days when all the other People held them up next to the Gods but I alone secretly did not pay them their due respect.

How strange it is that sometimes things reverse themselves. Odd that I, who once did not believe, had become one of the Priests' followers. And odd that the People, who had once believed so fervently, now had lost their faith.

But I could not blame them. Because the sadness had come to live in our villages, because the years of no rainfall had come, because of the fire and the raids, all had changed. Unhappiness, misfortune, and death had done strange things to my People, making them focus their anger upon the High Priests, making them find blame.

Yet I could not find fault with the High Priests. The High Priests, even though they were more knowledgeable than the common man, were only men, just as the others. They could not change the course of our fate. Even the Sun Watcher's knowledge of the skies would not allow him to see what the seasons would next bring. He could not see clearly, perfectly, into that blank future. He worked and toiled and worried over his duties just as the farmer and hunter did. But neither he, nor I, nor the Priests, nor anyone else, could truly claim that the days of happiness and prosperity would return to us again.

All of my remaining hope rested on the Stand Still Moon. Surely such a rare event would bring good fortune back to us. Later, as I sat with my father inside the pithouse where I was born, we spoke of it again.

"When will it come?" he asked me.

I answered, "Soon. Already the Moon has almost reached her position in the sky."

Father stared into the ash of a burned-out fire in the pit. "We will wait," he said. "We will wait until after the Moon rises between our Twin War Gods. But if our fates have not changed by then, we must leave."

I gulped but found that my words to talk him out of it had disappeared on my tongue.

He said, "We must pick up whatever we can carry and leave along with the others."

Over the next days, several small parties and one large group of villagers, including most of the Village Priests did abandon their homes. Leaving some of their elders behind, they gathered their most essential belongings and took to the trail down the river while warm weather still prevailed for traveling. By the time the Moon had almost reached the space between the Twin War Gods, already so many of our People had left, those remaining behind had gathered to live together in only one village, the village by the ravine. There one of the men always stayed awake to guard the village from intruders, and boys took turns watching the remaining cornfield all night long.

By the time of the Stand Still Moon, all of the People had grown so tired from work, worry, and from constantly standing guard, that few stayed awake long enough to witness the event. But I would not miss it. I stood with my brother Jumping Fish, along with a few others, on the top of the triangular mesa, home of the Great House. Together, we watched the great silvery Moon lift herself up slowly inside the space between the two rock towers, our Twin War Gods, sending bright rays of silvery light down to bathe our faces.

As she rose, I felt the smile come back to my face, and I held my brother's hand in mine and prayed for the People. Let this be the signal of safer, happier times to come. Let the good fortune of years past return to us.

"It has come," I said to my brother.

"Yes," he said, but I noticed how he lowered his eyes when he spoke to me.

"You do not believe in the power?" I asked him.

Jumping Fish gazed back at the full Moon. "I do not know what we are to believe any longer. Sometimes I believe only in full streams and green, growing crops. I believe only what I can touch with my hands and chew with my teeth."

I swallowed hard. "Let us see what the Stand Still Moon brings."

"Yes," Jumping Fish said as his expression lightened a bit. "Let us see."

After the Moon rose high in the sky, I returned to my room to describe the event to the Sun Watcher. He had decided earlier not to witness it, even though I had urged him to come outside if only to hear me describe the Moonrise and to feel the Moon's rays light on his face. But on this night, he felt too weak to climb the ladder out of our room. As I spoke to him and described the moonrise, I fashioned a sacred paho using down feathers from a wild turkey tied with a string of cotton—a thread between us and the Gods.

After I told my husband what I had made, he said, "Your choice is wise. Place it on the shrine at the base of the Twin War Gods to show our appreciation for the Stand Still Moon."

The next day, after I placed my paho on the rock shrine, I walked to the river for water. As I passed through the village by the ravine, I noticed another family packing their belongings as if to leave. Quickly I set down my water jar and hurried to my family's pithouse. Jumping Fish stood outside with our father, and when I saw him, I sensed that something else not known to me had happened.

"The one remaining cornfield," our father said before I had the chance to speak, "the only one not burned is beginning to turn brown and curl up and die."

I could not believe it. "But we have had rain," I almost shouted. "How is that possible?"

"Perhaps it was damage from the fires," Father spoke softly. "Perhaps the smoke has done it."

I gulped hard.

Jumping Fish took my arm and led me away from our father, away from others' watchful eyes. Then he abruptly stopped and turned me around to face him. His eyes were afire with the desperation that now seemed to live in his heart. "We must leave. We must take whatever corn can be salvaged from the fields and leave this place now, while Father and Grandmother are still strong enough to make the journey."

I nodded.

"You must come with us," he said.

I shook my head. "The Sun Watcher cannot make such a journey. During this winter past, his vision left him entirely, and the bone disease is so severe that now he can barely walk at all."

"I wasn't thinking of the Sun Watcher. I was thinking of you."

At first I could not move. Then I shook my head. He could not mean to suggest it. "I could not leave him here alone."

"You must, Echo. Or else you will perish with all the others who have no choice but to remain behind."

Again I shook my head as his meaning dawned on me. "No, brother. I will not go. I will not break the promise that I made to my husband on the day I married him."

"Tomorrow we harvest the raw green corn. Then at the next sunrise, we will leave." He squeezed my arms between his fists. "Go home tonight and pray to the Stand Still Moon that is your birthright. Listen to the Gods as you have never listened before, and do as you must do. Go with us away from this place."

I looked at the dust that covered my worn yucca sandals.

Jumping Fish startled me with the strength of his next words. "Are you listening to me, Echo?"

I nodded.

"Will you go?"

I did not answer, and for the first time in my life, my brother was angry with me. "I cannot talk to you any longer. For now, I must walk away. There is much work to do before we can leave."

I nodded again.

"Go and see our father," said Jumping Fish over his shoulder. "Maybe he can change your mind."

But I could never have seen my father. I could never have said goodbye.

That night, I heard that the High Priests had formed their own party intent also upon leaving soon. Together with some of the villagers that used to live along the eastern slope of the mesa, they would form another large party and abandon the Great House. Instead of going south and east, they had decided to travel south and west to a place they had once heard of back in the days when we were still visited by traders. A place not unlike our own home, a place of high mesas not far from mountains and woodlands. The other High Priests had given up hope even as the Stand Still Moon continued to rise between the Twin War Gods.

"It seems the power has left this place," the Sun Watch-er said to me that night as I told him of the news. "It seems we now live in a World out of balance."

And I could do nothing but agree with him.

16

LEAVINGS

The next day, I went to the field and worked alongside my brother, once again harvesting fields that had been tended with care over many years by the hands of my ancestors. Although it was not yet ready, we pulled the ears of corn from the dying stalks before they could fall to the ground. Children carried the ears to the village where the women tore away the cornhusks and inspected the ears to determine if any of it was fit to be cooked and eaten. They packed away the most mature ears of corn with them and then left the rest outside to rot or be eaten by rodents.

We pulled flat yellow narrow beans, speckled pinto beans, and hard white beans out of the ground, vines, roots and all. These we threw in heaps upon the ground and turned the vines and husks over and over until they dried. Later we trampled the vines to shake the beans out of their hulls, and then we swept up the beans with special brooms made of juniper boughs.

The women gathered up the remaining stalks and husks and burned them. Normally the ashes would be saved for use as fertilizer on next year's fields, but this year, as almost all the People were leaving, they allowed the ashes to blow away in the wind.

I could stand to watch no longer. Instead I ran to the river, to the place in the willows where once I had felt so carefree, where once I had sneaked away from my mother's watchful eyes and headed away on fine adventures in my favorite summer seasons. I stood there among the willows and waited for my breathing to slow. I fought away the tears, lest they steal down my face and turn me into a weak woman.

When I opened my eyes, he stood before me.

Falcon.

At first he was looking, only looking. His eyes were exactly the way I had remembered them. His face had changed, yes, had grown into the face of a full-grown man. But I saw that his eyes were still caves of black water. He looked at me softly, the same way he had on the day we spoke of marriage. I remembered all of it at once, our trio of adventure, the mischief we had gotten into in the days of our childhood, how Falcon's friendship with me had grown into something different and deeper, how I, too, one day in the depths of a canyon, realized that I loved him.

Falcon drew closer until he stood right before me. I had not been with him alone since the day we made our promises to marry each other. That day so long ago before everything was to change. After so much time apart and so much waiting, the points of light in my dream were now in front of me in solid flesh, and I thought I would be nervous. But I was not.

Then I remembered Red Rope, and I whispered her name.

"Do not speak of her, Echo, for she is happy among the good Cloud People."

Still I could not help remembering how joyful she had looked that day in the courtyard, that day soon after my marriage had given him to her, when she stood alongside her husband to be. Often I had wondered about their marriage, how he had heard the news of my marriage to the Sun Watcher, and if he had rushed to Red Rope. But I had only allowed myself the briefest moments to wonder because to linger in those thoughts had only caused me pain. Still during long cold nights I had wondered about them anyway over all the years of drought and sadness.

As if reading my mind, he began to tell me. Falcon said, in a whisper, "When I returned from the trading mission, no one, not even Jumping Fish, had the courage to tell me."

He drew in his breath as he continued, "For all of the first day, they could not meet my eyes. But I was so full of pride and happiness that I did not notice. I went around to all the People of our village and showed them the cotton cloth and the fine reed flute I had obtained in trade. You must know this: I had discovered a special flute, one that sends forth the most beautiful music I had ever heard, and all the way back from our mission, I had practiced playing it. I had practiced it long into every night so that I could play the Song of the Willows by the Waterside, so that I could play it for you."

As Falcon spoke, his words washed over me like warm water. There was something in his eyes, too, something like the flight of birds. His skin was darker and more drawn but it was still the face that I loved.

"Red Rope was a good friend and a good wife and a good mother. We had many moments of happiness. But this you must know: I never played the flute for her."

I closed my eyes at the pain and sorrow of his words. Red Rope.

"Do you understand what I am telling you, Echo?"

I looked up and let my stare settle in his eyes. "Yes."

Falcon now spoke in a bolder voice. "Tomorrow I take my son and begin a great journey."

My face fell. I had not thought of it until this moment arrived, but of course he would leave with the others.

"Once again, Jumping Fish and I will travel together. We will search throughout unknown lands until we find a place where faith once again holds true. Where rain will fall, where fields will grow, and where water will flow."

I bit my lip to keep it from quivering.

"All that is missing is you, Echo," he said. "You must come with us."

I looked straight into his eyes. "I cannot."

"You can and you must. Stay here and starve, or go with us and live."

I shook my head. "You are no longer married, but I am. And I made a promise to the Sun Watcher on the day our lives together began. He is a good man, Falcon. I cannot leave him here alone."

"I know that he is a good man. But he has lived a long life. And if you remain here," he said, furrowing his brow, shaking his head, "I cannot bear to think of what will happen to you."

"I can provide for us. Jumping Fish has taught me to trap and to throw the spear for wild game. I can plant small gardens below the mesa top."

"You don't understand what I am asking you, Echo. I am asking you to come with me. My wife is dead, and your husband is lost in that place between life and death. You and I are alive. Now we are given one last chance to be together, as we were always meant to be."

I looked into his eyes, searching for a way to make him understand. "Tonight the full Moon comes. Tonight she will rise again between the Twin War Gods. Tomorrow everything could change, everything could become better again."

Falcon looked away, and then he sighed and looked back at me. "No. It will not happen that way. We have waited long enough. It seems the Gods choose not to shine their light any longer in this place. It seems that the last gift given by the Stand Still Moon was many years ago. Her last gift was you."

Tears slid down my face and wet my neck.

"Come with us, Echo. Meet us at sunrise in the village by the ravine. Come away with your brother and your clan. Come away as my wife."

I did not speak.

"Do not answer me now. Think of it all night long and join us at sunrise, as you know you must."

I took Falcon's hand in both of mine, and as I touched his skin, I felt warmth enter the center of my body and felt all the smiles and laughter held back by so many desolate years well up within my throat. I held Falcon's hand between both of mine for only the time it took to take two more breaths, and then I turned and fled away, up from the river toward the mesa and the narrow causeway that led to the Great House.

I did not sleep that night. A night was never so long, and it was as though the morning was awaiting a great decision from me, one that required the turning of many thoughts and prayers as the stars rotated over our walls. But I did not wrestle with indecision, only with the guilt that there was a part of me that wanted to go. But my promise could not be broken, and even without the promise, I couldn't walk away from a kind old man who loved me.

In the morning, I took the Sun Watcher's sacred feather holder and great golden eagle feather, and I climbed to the highest wall of the Great House. There I stood and using the sacred feather holder, I chanted a special blessing for the travelers that the Sun Watcher had taught me long ago to pray.

I did not cry for I did not want to bring sorrow to their journey.

As I watched them leave, I saw steam from the hot pools down south on the river rise like the ghosts of elders released, and as the traveling party, including my family and Falcon, pulled away from my sight, fading away down the river road like tiny insects, I imagined the warmth of those hot pools. And I prayed that the travelers would find the big river that they sought far away to the south, and that her waters, the Gods willing, would be just as warm.

17

THOSE LEFT BEHIND

On the following day, the last band of travelers left along with all of the remaining High Priests, except for the Sun Watcher and the Priest married to my friend, Pond Lily. As Pond Lily was now days away from bringing her child into this World, they had decided to remain behind until after the child came. But soon after the birth, as soon as the baby was strong enough, they planned to follow the trail south and west to find the others.

We were few in numbers. The only ones left were the elders too weak to leave and Pond Lily, her husband, and me. As the last band of travelers went down the trail that followed the river, again I climbed to the highest wall of the Great House on top of the mesa. I watched and prayed my blessings upon them as they left. I watched as the last families and Priests and able-bodied elders walked away from the place that had been our home for many generations, as they left the ground where our People, young and old, had been buried over seasons of many other Stand Still Moons. Overhead, the Sun Father's disease spots remained on his face, a signal to us all that, for reasons we did not understand, our World was sick. Our World had lost her soul.

Back in the room I shared with the Sun Watcher, I worked on making a cradleboard for Pond Lily's child to come. I took two oval rings of willow I had earlier collected and tied them together, one above the other. Then I laid strips of juniper across, between the willows, and fastened them to the frame. Then I made a rabbit fur diaper from one of my blankets.

As I worked I felt a strange presence between us in the room.

"You are saddened," the Sun Watcher said.

"The others have left."

He sighed. "I see." He drew his legs slowly up under his blanket. "You should have gone with them."

"There are no hunters left to hunt the forests. There is no tribute to be paid to the High Priests, and the food stores are eaten away. The turkeys have starved, or been slaughtered, or have been taken along with the traveling parties."

The Sun Watcher sat very still. "I am an old man. Perhaps it is time for me to die, to die alone."

I shook my head. "We made an agreement on the day I became your wife, and that agreement I intend to keep. You have taught me knowledge of the stars and skies, and for that, I will care for you kindly until you die."

The Sun Watcher smiled. "Ah, yes, I remember. Even on that first day we met, you were wise enough to crave knowledge more than all else. For your wisdom, someday you will be rewarded and revered, young one."

I did not care about being rewarded or revered. All the thoughts that entered my head on that day were of finding food, staying warm, surviving. I worried about how I would care for those elders left behind, who had now moved into the Great House to be near me. Every day I had to travel farther and farther away to hunt game and to find wood for our fires. Every day the land seemed to have less to give.

"I have seen it in my dreams," he continued. "Someday, you will find your family again. You will lead them and those they travel with. You alone will know how to read the skies, how to study the horizon and determine a calendar, how to determine the correct days for planting and for harvest. You will be able to find the true directions so that the homes they build will set rightly upon the Earth."

But I did not answer. I could not tell the Sun Watcher that finally I, too, had lost my faith in his visions. I respected him for the knowledge he had given me about the skies, but the dream visions, I thought, came only from his hopes or his imagination.

Two days later, Pond Lily struggled to bring forth into this world a fine, fat boy infant. Without her mother there to help her, I came instead to her side and called out the chants that assured a safe entry into our World for the child. After his birth, the red-faced boy-child screamed and flailed his arms about, letting us know that he would be strong. Pond Lily and I both began to laugh, for even in this place of desolation, where all except a few, too unfit to travel, remained behind, still we had found a moment of rejoicing.

I took the baby from Pond Lily, bathed him, and rubbed him with juniper ashes to protect him from witches and evil Cloud People. Then I placed him on a bed of sand and put a perfect ear of corn, his Corn Mother, which Pond Lily had been saving in a hidden place for this occasion, beside him in the warm sand. Then for twenty days afterward, I kept both mother and child in their rooms away from strong light. Every fifth day, I washed Pond Lily's hair with yucca suds and bathed her in water in which juniper twigs had boiled.

"We have chosen a name for him, Echo," Pond Lily said to me one day as I washed her hair. "We will give him the name you were given on your twentieth day. Born of the Stand Still Moon."

"I hope the name will give him good fortune," I answered.

Pond Lily smiled. "I hope only for it to give him the same strength that it gave you. For if only he can grow to be as strong and wise as you, Echo, then all other things will come his way. Of this I am certain."

At sunrise on the boy's twentieth day of life, Pond Lily and her husband took the child to the highest point on the mesa top and dedicated their child to the Sun Father as he rose up over our World. Pond Lily held her newborn out to the east, to the south, to the west, and to the north, as far as her arms could stretch, and to all the Four Corners of the World, she said his name.

I gave to Pond Lily the fine necklace my husband had given me shortly after our marriage began, for certainly I would not need it any longer. I sent the gray dog away with her so that she could have a friendly companion on her journey. Then before the sunlight fully burned away the mists that rose over the river, they left, just as the others had left before them.

That night I did not cry for my friend because to do so might have brought her hardships. So I cried instead for the gray dog.

18

SOUTHERN WIND

Winter came, and with its snow, frost, and cold wind came a sickness that killed the remaining elders who had come to live with us in the Great House, those left behind. Until the moments of their death, I fed them as best I could and kept them warm. Then, upon their passing away from this life, I carried their bodies and buried them in the trash heap as I had done years before for my brother. I alone conducted the four days of ceremony that would assure their safe arrival in the Otherworld.

Throughout that winter, the Sun Watcher did well. Instead of falling ill as the other elders had done, he seemed instead to regain some of the strength in his limbs. Some days he arose from his bed, and with my support, he hobbled around our room once more.

During the long winter nights, he told me stories again, something he had not done for many Moon seasons. He told me tales of the times when his visions had been true, when he had been revered as a sacred one, a seer of the future. As he spoke, he smiled.

He described to me the great city that once had been the Center of the World, that place of many towers and tiered houses and High Priests. Where fine masonry, intricate pottery, and shell jewelry were common. That place that, now, we had heard, was empty of human life, left only for the field mice to scuttle in.

For the remaining winter months, I dug gophers out of their holes and tracked coyotes for food. I boiled roots I pulled from the ground and gathered seeds and nuts left behind in vacant pithouses. As I left the Great House each day, often I paused and remembered.

This had been the place where important People once visited, some of them from far to the south, from the Center of the World. This had been the place where People came to worship in the kivas, where masked dancers twirled to the full Moon and sang chants for many long days and nights. Where the High Priests once had studied the sky.

I walked past the walls of fine masonry completed by my People, the best craftsmanship in the entire World. Past the fortress that had held itself up, straight and intact, against the sting of the first winter winds, the heavy man-rains of summer, the hailstorms of early autumn. A place of pride.

Or so it had been.

I walked down the narrow causeway of rock separating the mesa top and the Great House from the rest of the city, past the Guard House. I stepped down from the causeway and walked through the villages where the People of the clans once had lived. Past rows of homes that once rang with laughter and shouting, and once were filled with much activity—cooking in the fires, trading in the court-yards, ceremonies in the Great Kiva, and many small, broad hands preparing beans, corn, and squash during the harvest. I remembered the Songs of the Arrow Makers, the ceremonies held before large hunts, the bean-sprouting songs, and the endless prayers.

When spring came, I had to travel far away to the east of the mesa to hunt for larger game, and as I passed by the plots of land that once had been our clan's fields, I paused for a moment to remember how it had been. I closed my eyes and remembered the laughter and the hopes for each harvest, the games played behind tall corn stalks, the weight of a ripe, plump squash in my hands.

But I opened my eyes, and there before me, all I saw was the dry, dusty ground and some charred remains of wood left behind from the fire.

I walked past the fields and headed down a gentle slope that once had been a forest and was now a meadow dotted with tree stumps. I walked toward a narrow canyon that led to a dry creek bed. Farther east, I knew a natural spring existed, and there I hoped to find a doe that I could take down with my spear thrower for a large supply of fresh meat. Instead, as I walked, I noticed something else, something I had never expected to find out in a meadow that had never been used as a field.

Tiny corn plants. Spread out in random were several new shoots pushing themselves out of the ground. I stopped and knelt down for a closer look. Indeed that is exactly what they were: tiny corn plants.

I lifted my head into the breeze and felt its warmth brush my face. This meadow was located downwind from the fields that had burned. Perhaps the corn seeds had been blown this way by the fire-fed winds. Perhaps they had found a home in the soil only to begin to grow again, now that springtime was coming. I pushed away the soil from around the base of one tiny plant, and immediately I noticed something. The soil was deeper brown in color, its texture more moist and rich than the soil in the dry, dusty field from which I had just come.

Quickly I raked my fingers through the soil.

I remembered one of the prayers I had once learned from my father. "Give love to all things—People, animals, plants, and mountains, for the spirit is one. New Worlds will depend on which pathway we walk—on one of greed and comfort, or on one of love and strength and balance."

Perhaps we had been too greedy with our fields and with the land. Perhaps we had taken them away from their center of strength and balance.

My mind moved with clarity as I remembered the prayer. "Live simply, humbly, and in a balanced way for the sake of everything that lives—man, animal, plant, rock, and the sacred water."

Perhaps we had asked too much of our fields. Perhaps they had needed to rest too, just as we needed our rest at night, just as the Earth needed to rest during the long wintertime.

I crumbled the soft soil between my fingers.

Perhaps we needed to move our fields from one place to another, allowing them to rest for a season or more. Perhaps moving away and finding fresh fields were all a part of our Mother Earth's plans for us.

I let the soil fall back down to the ground, knowing that I had made a discovery of great importance. I raced silently down to the spring, and even though I did not hunt down a doe on that day, I could not contain the excitement that stirred inside me. I could not wait to return to the Great House and tell the Sun Watcher of my discovery.

I thought of it all day long, felt the truth of my thoughts as I had felt no others before them. But as the day slowly stole its warmth away, and as I finally lowered myself down into the room, I immediately saw that something was wrong.

The Sun Watcher lay curled up like an infant, and the color had drained away, out of his face. I knelt down close to him and saw that he still breathed, although very shallowly. I began to softly sing the chant that assured safe passage into another World, and as I did so, he took his last breath, one long, deep sigh that took with it the life force out of his worn old body.

The air of his last breath touched my face like the silky tips of feathers. I did not cry, for he had lived a long life, and I did not wish to dishonor his memory by showing myself to be a weak wife. Instead I finished my chanting song. I could cry later, alone, in the night and maybe then the Gods would not notice me.

Then I did as I had now done for so many others before him. I prepared the body as was dictated by our ancestors, and then I carried him down the causeway. I would not bury him in the trash heap, because the ground was now soft enough for me to dig an earthen grave. I took him close to my favorite spot, on a little rise above the willows in the river. And after I returned his body to the Earth, I realized that I was the only person left alive in this once enormous place. But strangely, this thought did not bother me. For once, I held no fears at all. Perhaps I would finally learn to listen to my own stillness.

After four days, after the Sun Watcher's spirit had left this world, after the village walls and walkways and court-yards rang only with echoes, I began to have the dreams. Never before had I experienced such vivid and colorful experiences as I slept. Each morning I awakened confused because of the powerful images that had flown over me, like fast moving clouds, during the long night. In the begin-ning, I saw only bright blue skies and fields growing tall with corn plants, and water—softly flowing water.

But as the springtime came into summer, I began to see more. During the day, surrounded only by the silence of an empty city and the sounds of new leaves brushing against each other in the soft cool winds, I tended to the corn plants that had sprouted in the open, newly created field, and I planted beans and squash from seeds I had found in the corners of abandoned storerooms. These I planted in between the corn plants. Each day, I watched the bean vines creep across the ground and the corn grow tall, as gentle rains periodically fell and fed them with moisture.

In the evenings, I returned to the Great House and made myself a fire to warm the room before I retired to my feather blanket, as the nights were still cold.

By mid-summer, even darkness could not steal the warmth, and the land grew lush with green color. Fields buzzed with life, and animals scampered over rocks all around me. Meadows that once had been cut of all their timber began to sprout new trees. I found an entire forest of tiny aspen trees in one meadow alone. Thanks to the spring rains, wildflowers grew in abundance. Bright yellow ones covered the fields; tiny blue ones and pink cups with yellow centers grew in the shade. The river nearly overran her banks, the first time I can remember such high waters since my days as a girl.

Truly, it was the best of all the summers I could remember.

At night, I began to see in my dreams the trail to the south and west of here, the one that my family had traveled upon as they had left this place. I could feel the warmth of the path below my feet and the touch of the air on my face. I saw the changes of land along the horizon. Each night in my dreams, I traveled further along the trail, past the point where I had ever hoped to travel before in my waking life.

In my sleep I traveled south until I had to climb again and reach a pass that would take me safely over the high mountain ridge that divided the waters of the land. Then in the longest dream of all, I climbed high over that pass and looked down into the valley of the big river, the one where I would find my family.

At first I did not understand the message held in my dreams. Certainly I was being given directions as to how to move on, to find my family. That was clear to me. But it seemed to me that I had also been the one destined by the Gods to stay, the only one left behind to worship the Twin War Gods, to ask for their favors.

I was confused, because it seemed I was meant to be in two places at one time. I had been given the visions in my dreams by the Gods as well. Although I had not asked for or wanted them, I had been given them. It was as if, immediately upon the Sun Watcher's passage from life, as he had breathed his last breath, the gift of visions had been passed on to me. But I was not certain that I wanted such a gift, for with it came many responsibilities. Surely the Sun Watcher's predictions had not always come true. Certainly at times he had been wrong and had to carry that burden.

In the summer as the crops of my field grew high in the air and thick on the ground, I had a dream of those fields far away. One night I saw my brother Jumping Fish walking with the tall corn, and I knew that those new fields would soon be used over and over again by my People, as we had always done before. I knew I must share my discovery. I must make certain that my People would not again make the same mistake.

That night, I dreamed of the horizon upon which I would map out the seasons.

As the time came to harvest my crops, I stood in the tall corn and wondered what I would do with all the food I had grown in the new field. If I were to stay, I would need to harvest, dry, and store the food for winter. But all that work would be unnecessary if I planned to leave. Instead, I could leave the field as it was and simply let the animals come to feast.

The next day I ventured out into the hills far away from home. I found the gentle slopes covered with pinyon nuts that had popped out of their cones and scattered all over the ground, thick as a winter blanket. Together with the squirrels and the chipmunks, I scampered about and collected the tiny brown nuts and cradled them in the fold of my apron. When I could carry no more, I headed back in the direction of the Great House, sampling the nuts as I went along.

I ate the nuts in the manner I had been taught as a young girl—to place the nut, hull and all, in one side of my mouth. Then I cracked the nut open with my teeth, swallowed the meat of the nut, and then spit the hull out of the other side of my mouth.

I remembered Grandmother teaching Jumping Fish and me to do it in this way, and that memory brought a smile to my face. As I walked onward, I remembered another thing Grandmother had told us on that day. "A good traveler leaves a solid line of pinyon hulls behind him on the trail, to show others where he has been."

For the rest of the day, I left my pathway strewn with pinyon hulls. And the next day, I began to weave a new pair of yucca sandals for my journey.

On the last night I slept in the Great House, a full Moon rose between the rock pinnacles that were our Twin War Gods. The pair of falcons that nested on the cracks and crevices of the rock towers flew that night. They flew through the brilliant moonlit skies and screamed the high piercing call that only a falcon can understand.

That night, I dreamed of him. I saw Falcon before the firepit and felt my presence warm in the room beside him.

The next morning, I packed my bow and arrows on my back and carried strips of dried meat in a pouch, food to nourish me throughout my travels. I placed the necklace of small blue beads once given to me by my father about my neck, a symbol of the ties to my family. I donned my new yucca sandals and set out upon my journey.

I walked away alone, in the shadow of the rock spires, the Twin War Gods my People worshipped for many generations. My eyes followed up the long lines of their arms stretched into the sky. I prayed my good-byes, and as I at last recognized the rightness of my decision, I came to see it another way. Perhaps the Twin War Gods needed their rest also. Perhaps they needed only to stand tall against the wind and release pebbles that no one would hear and to reign only over lands left to fallow and renew.

I walked away from the Twin War Gods, past the Great House, down the causeway, and through the villages. I walked last through the village by the ravine, past the roasting pits and storage cysts, the courtyards between houses where I had played as a child. Finally I stopped at the pithouse where I was born under another Stand Still Moon.

Before I took the last step in the village, before I left the last footprint of my People in this place, I paused to close my eyes. With me, the life force would vanish from this place, would live on only in the memories of those who had once lived here, relived only in the voices of the storytellers. I remembered back to those happy days when the future kept its secrets in the wind.

Odd that it should be I, Echo, not some great warrior or Priest. Just one lone young woman, not yet twenty years old, was the one who stayed when the others had gone on to new lands before me. I alone witnessed the final day of the People in this high and windswept place where the Twin War Gods gave strength to the World, where the fields once burst with corn and beans, where the water sang in streams.

Just one small woman of the Waterfall Clan.

I walked away and feasted on pinyon nuts, leaving a trail of hulls all through the villages and down the trails, lest I never forget from where I had come. There was a southern wind blowing that day. Lifting my head, I caught the sweet scent of sage and prickly pear cactus in my nostrils. It was a good sign, a good omen for the beginning of a journey. For today I would walk into the scents of the lands that I sought to find. Today I would find my way.

AUTHOR'S NOTE

The people of this book are currently called Ancestral Puebloans or the Anasazi, a word from the Navajo that means "Ancient Ones." Long before European explorers came to the Americas, the Anasazi constructed a great civilization that included the famous cliff dwellings at Mesa Verde and had as its center the ancient city at Chaco Canyon.

The city in this book is considered by most archeologists today to have been an outlier of the great Anasazi civilization with history of human occupation that probably dates back to A.D. 150–400. During the eleventh century, dramatic changes occurred, expressed in the building of the large pueblo, or the Great House, on the mesa top. Archeologists believe it was developed possibly as a religious center or as an astronomical viewing point.

Eighteenth century Spanish explorers called the twin rock pinnacles La Piedra Parada, meaning the upright or standing rock. Later, nineteenth century Americans named them Chimney Rock, the same name given to other natural landmarks throughout the west. The Native American name is not known; however archeologists have learned through the study of modern Pueblo Indians that such physical features are believed to be symbols of their religious deities. They believe, based on the study of remains at Chimney Rock, that the twin spires may have been regarded as earthly manifestations of the Twin War Gods, prominent in Pueblo religion today.

The Anasazi of Chimney Rock left over 700 years ago and left no written records. Therefore, knowledge of ancient life must be gained from other sources, including archeologists, historians, and ethnologists. Archeologists unearth and study evidence from the materials found in ruins. Historians have added knowledge by studying the records and observations made by early explorers about the Pueblo Indians they encountered. Ethnologists, who study in detail a group of living Indians, add much to the picture. Without the help of present day Pueblo Native Americans, we would have little knowledge of such things as religion and society.

Beginning about A.D. 1130–1135, the great Anasazi civilization began to collapse. By A.D. 1276, most of the Anasazi not only left their homes, they moved off the Colorado Plateau altogether. Possible causes of the abandonment include drought, disease, overuse of natural resources, overpopulation, and invasion by enemies. The Anasazi of Chimney Rock are thought to have ended their journey in the Gallina uplands in New Mexico northwest of present day Jemez Pueblo. Chimney Rock's homes and kivas fell into ruin.

The land under the paired pinnacles lay vacant for nearly five hundred years. Today, Chimney Rock is a National Archeological Area and is open to guided tours between May 15 and September 15. The rock towers remain a historic peregrine falcon eyrie, or nesting site. Next to the ruins of the Great House stands a fire lookout tower from which the falcons can best be viewed.

If you'd like to learn more about Chimney Rock and the archeological areas surrounding it, here are some suggestions:

In the Shadow of the Rocks: Archeology of the Chimney Rock District in Southern Colorado, by Florence Lister. University Press of Colorado, 1993.

Prehistoric Astronomy of the Southwest, by J. McKim Malville & Claudia Putnam. Johnson Books, 1993.

Indians of the Mesa Verde, by Don Watson. Mesa Verde Museum Association.

Indians of the Four Corners: The Anasazi and Their Pueblo Descendents, by Alice Marriott. Ancient City Press, 1996.

CREDITS

The drawing on page 91 is an adaptation of figure 8, page 14, of *Prehistoric Astronomy of the Southwest,* Johnson Books, Boulder, Colorado, 1993 and used with the permission of the publisher.

The drawing on page 135 of the spearthrower (atlatl) is an adaptation of the drawing on page 29 of *Indians of the Four Corners: the Anasazi and their Pueblo Descendants,* by Alice Marriott. Drawing by Margaret Lefranc, Ancient City Press, Santa Fe, New Mexico, 1996, and used with the permission of the publisher.

The cover photograph is used with the permission of Pictures of Record, Inc., Weston Connecticut.

ABOUT THE AUTHOR

Ann Howard Creel is the author of three previous award-winning young adult novels—*Water at the Blue Earth, A Ceiling of Stars,* and *Nowhere, Now Here*—and one adult novel—*The Magic of Ordinary Days,* which was produced as a major Hallmark Hall of Fame presentation. Her interest in ancient America was fueled when she lived and worked for two years on the Navajo Reservation in Chinle, Arizona. For more about Ann and to write to her, please visit her web site at http://www.annhowardcreel.com.